the KATE in BETWEEN

ALSO BY CLAIRE SWINARSKI

What Happens Next

the
KATE
in
BETWEEN

CLAIRE SWINARSKI

Quill Tree Books
An Imprint of HarperCollinsPublishers

Quill Tree Books is an imprint of HarperCollins Publishers.

The Kate In Between

Copyright © 2021 by Claire Swinarski

Library of Congress Cataloging-in-Publication Data
Names: Swinarski, Claire, author.
Title: The Kate in between / Claire Swinarski.
Description: First edition. | New York, NY : Quill Tree Books, [2021] |
    Audience: Ages 8-12. | Audience: Grades 4-6. | Summary: Twelve-
    year-old Kate becomes the face of an anti-bullying movement after a
    heroic act goes viral, but her world is turned upside-down when the
    truth about her involvement is revealed.
Identifiers: LCCN 2020052655 | ISBN 978-0-06-291270-1 (hardcover)
Subjects: CYAC: Bullying—Fiction. | Heroes—Fiction. | Middle
    schools—Fiction. | Schools—Fiction. | Friendship—Fiction. | Fathers
    and daughters—Fiction.
Classification: LCC PZ7.1.S9477 Kat 2021 | DDC [Fic]—dc23
LC record available at https://lccn.loc.gov/2020052655

Typography by David Curtis
21 22 23 24 25   PC/LSCH   10 9 8 7 6 5 4 3 2 1
❖
First Edition

For my mom,
who loves me through all my in-between moments

the KATE in BETWEEN

1

EVERY STORY HAS A VILLAIN, AND THE ONE IN THIS STORY IS ME.

I need to tell you that right off the bat. Look—all tales need a bad guy. In some books, it's obvious. In *Peter Rabbit*, you've got Mr. McGregor chasing the poor bunny through his garden with a pitchfork. *Harry Potter* has Voldemort; *Holes* has the Warden. But sometimes the villain is a little harder to see. Maybe it's a tornado, a person's own self-doubt, or a friend who isn't who you thought they were. Villains don't always walk around with signs that say *Evil* hanging from their necks, snatching up hopes and dreams.

In this story, the one you're sitting down to read, I am the bad guy. Okay? Just know that now. This is not a happy-go-lucky fairy tale where a beautiful princess gets rescued by a handsome prince and they ride off into the sunset. This is a story of good vs. evil, of expectations vs. reality, of cell phones vs. your own two eyes.

If you feel like I already gave away the ending, don't be upset. Surprises are great. Except for when they're not.

I once swore to Haddie Marks on a jar of fireflies that we would be best friends until the end of time, and I meant it. Haddie's parents owned the Starfish Center, the pool club on the east side of Madison. Since it belonged to Haddie's family, we got to go for free. We spent almost every summer afternoon there—from when we were in first grade and her mom made us wear life jackets, all the way up until the summer before seventh grade, when we'd mostly just dangle our feet in and watch Brett and Nico do cannonballs, splashing Taylor Tobitt and all her friends. The air always smelled like coconut sunscreen and chlorine, and we'd split boxes of Sour Patch Kids, talking about how the next school year was going to change things.

That summer, the summer between grades sixth and seventh, things had already started to shift; the air seemed to crackle with change. We'd see a commercial for back-to-school clothes and notice our sunburns starting to fade. Sometimes we felt so grown up, like when Haddie's mom let us have sleepovers in the rec room at the Starfish Center, which was right next door to Haddie's house. But other times, we felt like little kids. When Taylor and her friends put little stickers on their stomachs while they tanned, creating pale hearts to show off to each other, while Haddie and I ate hot dogs with extra ketchup, we felt tiny.

On the last Saturday night before school began, Haddie and I watched lightning bugs light her backyard on fire, twinkling and winking at us as the sun went down. Our hair was still wet from the post-pool showers, and we were starting to shiver in our cutoff shorts and giant sweatshirts. We couldn't help but take a mason jar from her mom's gardening shed to capture as many fireflies as possible, poking holes in the top with a pair of scissors. We were way too old for that, and I felt it, that summer: the feeling of being Too Old. But something about it felt right, taking those little sparks of light and holding on to them for as long as possible.

We brought our jar into the rec room. Almost as soon as we got our sleeping bags set up, fanned out in front of the old, crappy TV, it started to rain. First a little trickle, pitter-pattering on the windows, and then—*kaboom*—bursts of thunder and lightning so bright it illuminated our faces.

"What if seventh grade is totally different? What if we don't have any classes together?" asked Haddie.

"We'll have lunch," I said. Seventh graders had their own lunch period. Same went for eighth graders.

"But what about Spanish? I'll fail. You know I see those verb endings and have a mental meltdown." It was true.

"Then we'll do homework together at night over the phone." I laughed.

"But anything could happen. What if—?"

"Haddie! *Stop.* It's still summer."

"Not for long," she said. "And what if everything changes?"

Haddie had started to cling tighter and tighter to our friendship, as if she felt like I had one foot out the door. I didn't, then—at least, I don't think so. Maybe I did. Maybe something about seeing Taylor Tobitt French-braid her hair and laugh at the boys made me wonder what else was out there besides endless summer afternoons eating Sour Patch Kids with Haddie. But she was my best friend, Haddie, through thick and thin. If she needed promises, I would make them. I grabbed our mason jar of fireflies, putting a hand over the top. "I swear on this jar—"

"Of bugs?"

"Of these . . . majestic creatures of *light*, thank you very much. I swear on this jar and all that is summertime, Haddie Alta Marks will be my best friend for all eternity."

"Stop. You know I hate my middle name."

"May no powers of East Middle School separate us, and may our schedules be identical. If any forces dare to come between us, may they be cast to the bottom of Lake Mendota. And let us get straight As and meet new boys on the first day of school who fall madly in love with us. And may Taylor Tobitt and Brett Browning be cursed with the black plague. Ameneth." I gave the jar a shake, jolting a few bugs awake.

Kaboom. We both shrieked as another burst of thunder hit, jolting off the rec room power and leaving us in pitch-black darkness. We ran back to Haddie's house in the rain, the storm soaking our pajamas, laughing so hard we could barely breathe. We made a huge bowl of popcorn with an entire stick of butter melted on top once the power turned back on and watched a black-and-white Audrey Hepburn movie. Haddie fell asleep first, like always, and I suddenly started to feel bad about those stupid fireflies. We'd forgotten all about them. They didn't belong locked

5

up in a jar, scared and stuck. We could escape from the rec room, but they couldn't escape from their little prison. When the movie was over and it had finally stopped raining, I took the jar outside. I turned it upside down and shook it, letting the bugs fall to the ground. They stayed there for a minute, all dizzy, before finally flying away.

2

THERE'S NOTHING MORE EMBARRASSING THAN BEING DRIVEN to school in a cop car.

I scooted down as far as possible in my seat. It wasn't even one of those plain white, unmarked vehicles that hide around corners waiting for speeding teenagers to drive by. Nope, it was a good ol'-fashioned copper-mobile, with the words *Madison Police Department* in huge letters slapped across the side.

"This is humiliating," I muttered.

Dad glanced over at me and shrugged. "Sorry, Bird. These are my only wheels." Dad had a take-home car from the City of Madison so that he could be at work the minute he left his apartment. Just in case he had to pull over some speeding truck driver on the way to the station.

"I could have walked."

"What kind of dad would I be if I let you hoof it a mile and a half?"

"Mom let me," I muttered.

Dad sighed and pulled up to the school drop-off.

Okay, fine. It wasn't his fault I was stuck in an apartment that was a full mile farther away from school than Mom's rental had been. But it wasn't *mine* either.

We'd had this exact same conversation almost every single day for the past month. Ever since I came home from school to find Mom packing up our life, shoving things haphazardly into boxes, and found out that I'd be moving in with my dad.

My mom was a salesperson for True U Cosmetics. She sold lip liner and eyeshadow to other moms, convincing them to ditch their cubicles and offices for a life of #TrueFreedom. Sometimes, when things were going well, she'd get sweet perks: a cruise trip here, a bonus there, a FaceTime call with the company CEO, who praised Mom's team-building skills.

But when things weren't going well . . . we moved.

Key word: *we*.

We were always in search of a cheaper apartment farther away from the university's campus, one without bats, or loud undergrads raging on the floor above ours. But this time, she'd flown solo, dropping me at Dad's apartment building with a Truly Ruby–colored kiss on my cheek. She said she had to go "step into her spotlight"—the True U motto, proclaimed in sparkly letters on her Toyota Camry's bumper. She needed to go to Utah, where True U headquarters was expanding. More opportunity to recruit her downline, the women she taught to sell makeup and got bonuses from. There would be more opportunity for throwing home makeup parties where customers could be dazzled by the new deals on mascara, too, meaning more opportunity to Follow Her Dreams. Thanks to her hard work, she told me, there was a True Emerald on every block. Mom was a True Sapphire, the next rung up on the ladder. She was trying to get all the way to True Diamond, where you're given a True Tesla and are recognized at all the national conferences.

But I couldn't go. It was the middle of the school year and the basketball season, and besides, I didn't want to move to Utah. I tried to convince her to stay, insisting that I didn't care if she came to basketball games to sell mascara to other girls' moms and sisters. But it didn't work. She was moving out west, and I was moving in with Dad.

In one night, I had packed up my entire life. It's not like I had a lot of stuff—when you move as much as we did, it's easier not to haul tons of crap around.

Dad lived on the sixth floor of an apartment building, the kind with ugly hotel carpeting. The Windy Willow Brook apartment complex had just gained a new resident: me. I didn't even have a room, just a pullout bed in Dad's office.

Mom liked sudden things. Change of plans, spontaneous desserts, vacations taken without calling school to tell them I'd be gone. Schedules made her itchy—they weren't quite as fun as *dreams*, which she liked to scrawl out on her #GirlBoss whiteboard. Dad liked order, plans, and bullet points. Reason #87 on my I'm Not Sure How They Were Ever In Love list, but they must have been at one point. I have an old photo I love: it's the two of them in the school parking lot after prom, Mom's belly already big with yours truly, Dad's eyes happy and bright, their arms flung around each other. They just look . . . meant to be.

But I guess they weren't. I wasn't even a year old when they broke up.

My move happened four weeks ago, so you'd think I would have gotten used to riding to school in a police car. But it was still weird, every single morning.

I grabbed my backpack from the spot between my feet. I could have put it in the back seat if it hadn't been for the window of bulletproof glass blocking it.

"I have basketball practice after school," I reminded him. "Be home late."

"Got it. You need a ride?"

"*No.* Houa's mom can drive me." I shut the door as hard as I could before he had a chance to say no. Getting a police escort around town made me feel ridiculous.

"Hey," he said, rolling down the window as I bounded up the steps to school. "Have a good day. We can get ice cream from Ella's Deli after dinner tonight, okay? I love you."

"Are you bribing me with ice cream to try to put me in a good mood?"

"Is it working?"

I rolled my eyes. "Love you too."

"'*Love you too,*'" a falsetto voice squealed. I glanced over to see a group of eighth-grade boys snickering and punching each other. Dad cleared his throat loudly, and they shut up real fast.

I hurried into school before anyone else noticed.

"Kate!" Taylor waved to me from the lunchroom, where we hung out before first bell. She was with Violet and Amira, but also Nico and Brett. We had only just started sitting with the boys at lunch, and to be honest, I thought they were pretty annoying—fart noises and stupid jokes and making fun of everyone

11

who wasn't sitting with us.

"Hey," I said, throwing my bag down. Taylor was fixing her ponytail. She was white with blond hair, like me, but her hair was Barbie-doll-blond, while mine had the unfortunate name of dirty blond.

"Question," said Taylor.

"Answer."

"The math homework?"

"What about it?"

Taylor clasped her hands together and looked at me, eyes pleading. "I'll owe you a million homeworks after this."

I rolled my eyes. "I'm pretty sure your tab is already way higher than that." But I still pulled out my blue math notebook and handed it to her to copy.

"Tsk, tsk," said Nico, looking around. "I should tell Principal Howe we have some cheaters in our midst."

"I don't think Officer McAllister would approve," said Violet, smirking as she tied her long red hair into a French braid. I was always getting crap from Violet and everyone else about my dad being a cop. Back in first grade, when he came to our class to talk about wearing seat belts and not talking to strangers, he was a celebrity. Now it was just embarrassing.

"Ha, ha," I grumbled. "You're hilarious."

"Who peed in your Cheerios this morning?" asked Taylor, scribbling down my answers.

"Get a few of them wrong so we don't get busted," I said. "And nobody. I just . . ." *I just didn't sleep well because my dad's street is too loud and there's a creepy painting of Jesus staring down at me from the wall of his office, where I've been sleeping for the past month. And I wish you would do your own stupid homework, because this took me an hour last night.*

Taylor looked up at me, waiting.

"I'm tired," I said.

I hadn't exactly shared with everyone that I'd moved in with my dad. My parents were already different from everyone else's. The way my dad drove around town in his patrol car and looked young enough to still be in college. The way my mom's job involved annoying all the other moms at sports awards ceremonies and spelling bees, trying to get them to sell True U too. The way they both lived in apartments instead of houses with basements and pools and speakers named Alexa or Siri you could talk to. The last thing I needed them to know was that my mom had hightailed it to the other side of the country to chase after her dream of selling lip gloss.

"Hey, Kate," said a voice. I glanced up.

Haddie stood there, in a *Fort Wilderness* T-shirt and leggings with a hole in the knee. Her dark hair was down, wavy, and tumbling over her shoulders. She was wearing . . . weird animal earrings. What were those? Wallabies?

Brett coughed back a laugh, and Amira kicked him. Violet just smirked and watched me.

"Hey," I said awkwardly.

We all stood there, quietly, while Taylor copied my homework.

"Um, are you doing anything this weekend?" asked Haddie. "Because I thought, like, maybe—"

"Hey, Haddie?" asked Taylor, lifting her head from my notebook. A smile stretched across her face, but it wasn't a nice one. It was a Taylor smile, the kind that you need to watch out for.

"Yeah?" Haddie asked.

"You have something in your teeth," Taylor whispered extra loudly.

Haddie threw a hand over her mouth, her cheeks blooming bright red. She always did that when she got embarrassed, ever since we were kids. It didn't happen very often. Haddie wore what she wanted, did what she wanted, and said what she wanted. I was pretty sure that was why Taylor didn't like her.

The entire lunch table cracked up, except for me. Haddie turned around and quickly walked away.

"You're welcome," Taylor said to me.

The bell rang.

Homeroom meant Marks and McAllister sat right next to each other.

That was how we'd met, too, way back in first grade. Miss Troia sat us in alphabetical order, which left Haddie and me at the yellow table across from Thomas Miller, who ate glue, and Carlos Mejia-Thompson, who made lightsabers out of his erasers and spent most of the day making alien noises. We had no other option but to band together against the forces of Boy Cooties.

Six years old, seven years old, eight years old. Every birthday party and weekend sleepover. I went with her family on vacation to Denver one spring break, and she came on a celebratory Chicago weekend trip with us after Mom added four Emerald sellers to her team in a single month.

The Dynamic Duo, my mom called us, when Haddie and I spent hours last summer learning how to tie bracelets out of rope. We both made one that was blue, white, and gray—the colors of the lake—and gave them to each other. We were wearing them the night of the fireflies.

But that was before.

I slid into my homeroom seat.

"I saw your dad dropped you off today," said Haddie.

"Yup," I said, trying to look busy organizing notebooks in my bag.

"Is he driving you to school now?"

"Yup."

"How's Watson?" Watson was my dad's Westie. I guess now he was my dog too. Watson was much happier about it than I was. This morning, he trotted over to me excitedly, leash in his mouth, as if I was available 24/7 to be his fitness partner. Having a dog, like so many other things, sounded a lot better in theory. Kind of like living in an apartment with your police officer dad and sleeping in his office.

No, wait—even *I* know that sounds crappy.

"Good," I bit out. I felt myself tighten up. I hated that Haddie knew details about my dad's apartment, like the fact that he had a dog. I didn't want to talk about my dad's place. I didn't want to talk about anything. But Haddie was the kind of friend who actually asked you about your life, which made me want to be as far away from her as possible.

The truth was, Haddie's family was just—is *perfect* too cliché? That's what they were, though. Her parents took *ballroom dancing* together. She lived in a giant brick house next to her family's pool, the kind that people walking by would stop to look at. For so long, it had felt like differences didn't matter between us. *Yeah, whatever, your family is kind of rich and mine isn't, ha, ha.* Haddie had never minded coming over to Mom's apartment, wherever it happened to be at that moment. But something about it felt weird now.

It wasn't that Haddie wouldn't understand. It's that she would. And that look in her eyes when she saw things like my mom's True U posters—that look of *Kate, I'm sorry your mom is so weird*—I didn't want to see it anymore. I didn't want to show her the Windy Willow Brook apartment complex and see her sympathetic eyes and hear her asking me if I wanted to talk about how hard it was to move. I just wanted to pretend like none of this had happened at all.

The bell rang and Mrs. Urbanski clapped her hands together to quiet down a group of boys arguing about a college basketball game the night before.

"Mrs. Beyoncé," Haddie whispered to me, grinning. We used to call Mrs. Urbanski that because she looked exactly like Haddie's favorite singer, Beyoncé, if she had decided to take a totally different career path and become a middle school pre-algebra teacher. I gave a half smile and looked ahead. It was like no matter how many weeks went by, she wasn't going to get the message that we weren't best friends anymore.

"Listen up, everyone," said Mrs. Urbanski after a quick run-through of the pledge. Haddie always remained seated—she never thought twice about standing out, about doing something that would make people look at her. "There are a few announcements before the day gets rocking and rolling here. First of all, mock-trial team members, don't forget that we have a competition in McFarland tomorrow, so you'll need to get here at seven a.m. sharp to hop on the bus. Also, the bleachers are being painted this afternoon, so gym will be in the cafeteria and there's no basketball practice or dance team after school. We don't want anyone inhaling poisonous paint fumes."

Sweet. I liked basketball, but a surprise afternoon free of Coach Watt barking at me sounded pretty good.

"Cool," said Haddie. "Want to hang out tonight? You could come over."

For half a second, I almost said yes. I mean, I had no excuse—practice was canceled. And she looked so *excited* at the idea. Maybe for just one afternoon,

I could go back to Haddie's house, and we'd eat raw cookie dough and hang out in her bedroom, laughing about dumb stuff Taylor had said. Haddie still had her bracelet on, the blue-and-white-and-gray rope one. I hadn't worn mine in a while.

Haddie and Kate, Kate and Haddie. It was tempting, but—

My phone buzzed and I glanced down at it. It was a text from Taylor.

No dance team tonight. 🙌 Hang out after school?

Taylor was on dance team with Violet and Amira. Almost everyone at our school did something after the final bell rang. Principal Howe was kind of obsessed with extracurriculars. It was like if we didn't sign up for student council or a sport, we were destined for a future of failure.

What was I supposed to do? Say no to Taylor because I had to go hang out with Haddie Marks? It would be a joke for weeks. Taylor had some kind of thing against Haddie. If I waved to Haddie in the hallway, I heard about it from Taylor for the rest of the day.

"I can't," I said. "I'm hanging out with Taylor."

"Oh," she said.

"Sorry," I said awkwardly. But she'd turned back to the front of the classroom. And there it was, a blooming guilt that took root in my stomach like a weed every time I broke a promise I'd made over some fireflies.

The day flew by. We had a substitute in Spanish who didn't speak Spanish, so we watched *The Lion King* dubbed in Spanish, with English subtitles. I asked if I could go to the library to work on my English paper instead. The sub shrugged, so I took that as a yes and showed him where Señora De La Rosa kept the passes.

But once I got to the library and hopped on a computer, I didn't open my paper on symbolism in *The Giver*. Instead, I glanced over my shoulder at Mr. Kim, the librarian. He was about as passionate about books as I was about *The Lion King*, so why he became a school librarian, I wasn't exactly sure. As he was in the middle of trying to keep a rowdy group of sixth graders focused on their research project, I pulled up the True U website.

Unlock Your True Potential in Five Easy Steps, the latest blog post said. I clicked on it, thinking maybe I should send it to Mom so it could whisper the secrets of unlocking Diamond in her ear.

"Kate? Aren't you supposed to be in class?"

My eyes shot up. It was Mr. Collins, my English teacher.

"We have a sub for Spanish," I said, "and he no hables español."

Mr. Collins winced at my grammar. "Neither do you, apparently."

I grinned. Mr. Collins was one of those teachers who *got* kids. English class was my favorite part of the day.

"What are you working on? Tell me it's not the paper on *The Giver* that's due tomorrow. You should be in final edits."

"No," I said honestly.

"Some other secret work of genius, I presume? Remember, the *Knightly News* is always accepting new writers."

The *Knightly News* was East Middle School's news blog. They wrote about the fascinating goings-on at our school, like the freshly painted parking lot or the hiring of a new lunch server. Real hard-hitting stuff. Mr. Collins had been trying to get me to join all year. He was constantly telling me I was good at writing. But the *Knightly News* was kind of dumb, and besides, I had basketball after school every day. I was the tallest girl on the team—Coach Watt would kill me if I quit.

"I've told you a million times: I'm not a real writer," I said. Mr. Collins might have given me good grades on English papers, but it wasn't like I was some journalist.

"I think you have me mistaken for Karlie." Karlie Filing was one of those girls who just screamed "writer." She was always doodling lines of poetry on her forearm and volunteering to read her work in class. She once gave Haddie and me dirty looks for reading *Percy Jackson* during free reading as she pulled out *Pride and Prejudice*.

Mr. Collins laughed. "I'll see you in English class, Kate. And hopefully at a *Knightly News* meeting one of these days."

As he walked away, I snuck another look at the librarian's desk to make sure Mr. Kim wasn't about to bust me for unauthorized computer usage. But he was busy talking to someone handing him a sheet of paper—Haddie, who was an office aide fourth period. A few months ago I would have jumped up, thrilled to see my best friend in the middle of the day. But now everything was different.

I don't know what changed. It's not like I could pull out a calendar and point to a day when Haddie and I stopped hanging out. We were just so different. Things that had seemed small and unimportant suddenly started to seem bigger and bigger.

When we first got to East Middle back in sixth grade, she wore these sparkly lion earrings every day.

Whenever anyone asked about them, she'd go off into this whole speech about lions becoming endangered, even though, hello, we live in Wisconsin. Not exactly spotting Simba outside. Like, really? Could you at least try to fit in a little bit? Her anime drawings, which used to seem kind of impressive to me, now just made her stick out. Everything Haddie did was so . . . loud. So out there. Like she didn't understand the importance of being normal. I spent sixth grade with my head down, just being a person in the crowd. All I wanted to do was blend in, which is hard enough when you're my height. But everything about Haddie shone a spotlight on us. Her uniqueness was the determined kind that couldn't easily be squashed, no matter how hard people tried.

At the beginning of seventh grade, Ms. Irvine had assigned our science class lab partners. Everyone knows that teachers get some kind of sick pleasure from pairing you with a partner you don't want to be with. But some small part of me was glad when I was put with Taylor Tobitt. Taylor didn't draw anime or wear animal earrings. Taylor . . . well, Taylor didn't do much of anything, to be honest. She spent a lot of time on her phone. I didn't really know why, but everyone wanted to be her friend. Except Haddie and me, who had spent most of sixth grade rolling our eyes at her.

"Hi," I'd said awkwardly, pulling up a stool to our lab station. "I'm Kate." Of course, I knew who *she* was, but we'd only had one class together the year before, and we'd gone to different elementary schools. I assumed she had no idea who I was.

But she surprised me.

"I know," she said.

"You do?" I asked.

"Yeah," she said with a smile. "Your mom . . . your mom does the makeup thing, right?"

My face got hot. Of course. Of *course* Taylor Tobitt would know my mom was the True U lady.

"Amira's mom went to a party of hers last year, and your mom asked if we knew you," Taylor said smoothly. "Do you know Amira and Violet?"

"Yeah," I said. The three of them were best friends.

"Amira's mom bought a foundation and it made her skin break out," said Taylor.

I could have killed my mother.

"Do you get free makeup from her?" she asked, completely ignoring the fact that we were supposed to be looking at a leaf under a microscope.

"Yeah," I said. "All the time." Well, that part was true. Not that I wore any of it. It was mostly sitting in boxes, and it wasn't *really* free—Mom often had

24

to buy in bulk in order to keep her status, and then try to sell her stockpile to people at in-home parties. Some people kept their car in the garage; Mom kept shelves of blush.

"Hmm," Taylor said. I couldn't tell if she thought it was cool—*free makeup*—or weird—*will give your face a freaky rash*. Then she glanced at where Ms. Irvine was working with a group and pulled out her phone to start texting.

So it wasn't friendship at first conversation.

"Ugh, sorry you're stuck with Taylor," Haddie told me that day at lunch. I usually brought mine from home, but Haddie bought hers at school—some kind of weird, gooey meat over rubbery-looking noodles.

"How can you eat that?" I asked, wrinkling my nose.

"What?" she asked, shoveling a forkful into her mouth.

A table burst into laughter. I looked over and spotted Taylor's messy blond bun, Violet's red braid, and Amira's yellow headscarf, all three of them leaning over and looking at something on Violet's phone.

"They're annoying," said Haddie. "I'm with Roger for science lab. He's so funny. We're going to make a lightbulb for the science fair."

"Hmm," I said, not really listening.

"What did you and Taylor even talk about? Makeup?"

"What?" I asked, my eyes fiery. "Is that supposed to be some joke about my mom?"

"What? *No*," Haddie said, shaking her head. "Geez. I just meant that Taylor likes makeup."

"Oh. Yeah. Duh," I said, still only half paying attention. "I mean . . . Taylor's not so bad."

"Uh, yeah she is," said Haddie, rolling her eyes. "I bet she thinks photosynthesis is just an app you can use to add filters to your selfies."

But Taylor was actually pretty smart. She pulled her weight on our lab assignments, at least. And the more we sat together, the more I liked her. I liked that she knew things about different kids at school and would tell me in a whisper—that Rachel Hyatt's older brother was in jail or that Carmen Cortez and Tony Doyle had kissed at Carmen's boy-girl birthday party. I liked that she always had a new singer she was into and that she would play me their songs. And I liked that she was funny, even though her funniness was sometimes mean.

After being Haddie's friend for so long, it was kind of nice to be around someone like Taylor. She'd just *say* things, anything she wanted—like that Isla St. James's hairdo looked like Princess Leia's, or that Mr. Becker, our history teacher, always smelled like soup. That meanness was so different from Haddie's always-goodness, or Mom's constant rah-rah-sparkle vibe. But it made me feel . . . I don't know. Included. Like, if I was talking *with* Taylor, I knew she wasn't talking *about* me. And I didn't have to try to step into any spotlight. I could just bask in Taylor's.

One day, we had to stay in Ms. Irvine's room past the bell to finish up a lab assignment. We'd spent too much time talking about Taylor Swift's new album and not enough time filling out our lab results. I'd waved to Haddie as she left class and told her I'd see her later.

But after, when we walked into the cafeteria and saw Haddie in the lunch line waiting to buy her mystery meat, Taylor had grabbed my arm.

"Kate," she said. "Come sit with us."

I glanced at Haddie in line. Then at Taylor. Then back at Haddie. And I asked myself who I really wanted to sit with. I'd had a bad day—Mom had been arguing with Dad on the phone late into the night, and I hadn't been able to sleep, so everything felt groggy. I just wanted to do something that would make *me* happy, for one lunch period. For one stupid half hour, I wanted to choose myself. I didn't want to pretend to be into anime when I wasn't, or act like I thought Taylor was some big jerk when I didn't. Did I really want to hear more about

Roger's science puns, or Haddie's cat, Franz, who was always going to the vet for something or other? Or did I want to be invited to Carmen Cortez's next boy-girl birthday party? It felt like a big choice, and I wanted to make the right one.

So I sat with Taylor. And I guess if I had to point to a moment, that was it. Because Haddie walked over to the lunch table where we usually ate and sat alone, looking over at me occasionally, as I avoided eye contact. And that was where I sat, from then on.

Taylor invited me to her house the very next weekend.

Taylor's house was so different from mine. She had a TV in her room, and her dad left us totally alone. Unlike my mom, who always wanted to hang out with me and Haddie and talk. Plus, the Tobitts usually had soda in their fridge—the real stuff, not the generic kind that only came in big bottles. She had a fireplace we could turn on as it got colder and fall started to slide into snow. We could do whatever we wanted on her laptop with nobody looking over our shoulders.

I just loved sitting in her bright purple bedroom, knowing I was in *Taylor Tobitt*'s room, being included. I loved feeling *chosen*. I loved when Taylor tagged me in an Instagram post and everyone saw it and thought,

Wow, I wish I was as lucky as Kate McAllister. At least, I imagined they did. Because that was what *I* spent years doing, even as I laughed alongside Haddie at Taylor's super-tight jeans or her loud fake giggle. Who knows why people like Taylor see things in people like me? I don't. There's a lot of stuff I don't know. That's just the way the world is.

So I had moved lunch tables. The energy had shifted—the kind of shift where things can't ever go back to how they were, not really. But after that, there were a million smaller moments that pushed Haddie and me to where we were now, fractures that in the moment could've been played off as not that big a deal. I didn't go to Haddie's on Halloween for a scary-movie marathon with her, her mom, and her big sister like I always had. Instead, I was invited to Amira's house for a sleepover. During winter break, Haddie called almost every day to see if I wanted to come over for hot chocolate and Netflix Christmas movies, but I ignored her calls in case Taylor wanted to do something, which she usually did.

On the last day of our holiday break, Taylor and I went to the mall because she needed a new pair of jeans. As we left Hollister—Taylor clutching three bags—and headed to meet my mom, who was doing some work in the Barnes & Noble café, I saw Haddie across the walkway with her sister. We stopped and looked at each other. She raised a hand and waved at me, and I could have sworn I saw tears in her eyes. I waved back, but then Taylor yanked me away.

Haddie texted me that night, after we saw her at the mall: *I don't get it. Where did you go?* I know she didn't mean where I went that *day*, walking out of Hollister and past Pottery Barn. She meant where I had gone, from being her best friend to being someone who ignored her.

I didn't answer.

I missed Haddie every now and then, like on days when I wanted to go to school in old sweats without Taylor making some joke about how I looked like my dad had just picked me up from jail. Or when I wanted to read without Taylor making fun of my library choices because she thought any books that weren't megapopular were weird. (Harry Potter was fine because everyone had read those. But random historical fiction books? No go.) And sometimes I simply missed, well, who Haddie *was*, and the comfort of being with someone you know inside and out.

Kate and Haddie, Haddie and Kate. The Dynamic Duo was no longer. That firefly promise of friends forever had been a lie I told. Not my first, and not my last.

It wasn't as if I suddenly didn't like Haddie, or that I wanted her to be sad. I just loved being in Taylor's world.

Most of the time.

SINCE I DIDN'T HAVE BASKETBALL THAT AFTERNOON, I HUNG out with our usual group after school: Taylor, Violet, and Amira, and Brett and Nico, who had tagged along at the last second. We were outside, since it was surprisingly warm for a February day in Wisconsin. The day before, we'd had a Winter Weather Advisory, but that was the Midwest: you'd need a pair of gloves and sunscreen all in the same day.

I didn't know how important that afternoon would be when I wore my too-small bright purple spring jacket. But not having to haul out my heavy winter coat had felt like a minor miracle.

"Not going to lie, I love not having to spend the afternoon with Miss London yelling at me about straight legs," said Amira. "Are you stoked not to have basketball?"

I nodded, but the truth was, I usually liked basketball

fine. I had one job on the team: rebounds. I was the tallest girl in school, and Coach Watt had hounded me until I agreed to join the team. My job was to stand under the basket, every game, and catch the ball after other players missed, before passing it to our best shooters.

"It's so nice out today." Taylor stuck her face toward the sun, shutting her eyes. We were by Woodglen Pond, which had a trail that wrapped around it. It was pretty close to Taylor's house, so we'd probably stop there afterward. We were bored and full of energy, and that early-spring sunlight made us want to be anywhere outside.

"You look like a cat. The way they always find the sun," I said with a laugh.

Poking fun at Taylor could be a risk—you never knew if she was going to laugh or get ticked. But she clawed the air and let out a meow, which cracked us up. She leaned over and tried to lick my cheek, and I laughed, swatting her away.

"Let's take a picture," she said with a giggle. "Here, Violet—can you take it?"

Violet froze. "Um . . . sure."

Taylor handed her the phone and pulled me in tight. Our cheeks pressed together, the sun shining in our eyes—I could barely see Violet's and Amira's looks of hurt as the phone clicked.

"Hey," said Brett, "isn't that Haddie Marks?"

And there she was, on a walk by herself. Haddie was always doing things like that and not caring how weird it was. She had just turned a corner of the trail and was heading right toward us, coming out from behind a thick row of trees.

"Haddie," Nico called out. She looked up and froze, like a deer who'd been spotted. Then she saw me and relaxed a little.

"Hi," she said nervously, slowing to a stop, as if she were going to join us.

"Nice hat," said Taylor. Violet, Amira, Brett, and Nico cracked up. It actually *was* a cute hat. Pink and knit, with a silver pom-pom hanging off the end of it. Very Haddie. But Taylor's compliments: they were never what they seemed. She'd just pick something and go after it. Even though . . . it was a *hat*. How come when Taylor wore hats, it was cute, but when someone she didn't like wore one, it was something we should all laugh at? Sometimes I felt like we all needed a flow chart of Acceptable Clothing or something.

"Thanks," Haddie said, making everyone laugh harder. *Haddie, stop*, I wanted to whisper. We were all together now, close enough that I could see her eyes,

34

a mix of cautious curiosity and slight annoyance. I wished she'd realize they were being jerks and accept it—just walking away would be so much easier for her. She made everything harder on herself. I wanted her to wake up and see how the world reacted to her, to someone who wore whatever she wanted and didn't care about Taylor Tobitt's opinion. To someone who asked bizarre questions about the dietary restrictions of the Aztecs in history class. To someone who went door-to-door on Earth Day and handed out flyers on recycling. Why were these things so clear to everybody but her?

"Can I see it?" asked Violet. Or was it Taylor? *Someone* reached their hand out, and Haddie looked at me, with no idea what to do.

Take a joke. That's what Taylor would say. Always reminding people she was *kidding.* It was *funny.*

I laughed. I tried to make it sound nice, but even I heard how it came out—mean, cutting, and loud. And *not* like I was on Haddie's team at all. It was a Taylor laugh, a new language I was apparently fluent in.

Haddie took off her hat and handed it to Taylor.

"Catch," Taylor said to Nico, throwing it his way. And that's when Haddie realized: Taylor wasn't trying the hat on. We weren't on her side. This was mean, *actually* mean, and she was one against six. Nico threw the hat to Violet.

"Give it back," Haddie said quietly. "I have to get going . . ."

"Where?" said Violet, tossing the hat back to Nico. "To hang out with all your friends?"

"Violet! Geez," said Amira. But she was smiling.

Like an attack dog who's torn free from its leash, Violet kept going. "Nobody wants to hang out with you," said Violet. My chest tightened. This was all too much, and so fast. She sounded so . . . *angry*. We had just been hanging out, feeling the sun on our faces, but suddenly, we were tumbling faster and faster toward some kind of inevitable conclusion I didn't want to see at all.

"That's not true," said Haddie, her voice cracking a little. Because *not caring* can only go on for so long, and it was pretty clear that Haddie's *not caring* was getting tired.

"You guys—" I said.

"What, Kate?" snapped Taylor. Everyone stopped and looked at me. It was a test, and I was failing.

I had to pick where I belonged, but I had no idea how.

Nico threw the hat back to Violet, who threw it to Amira. Haddie started crying, running after whoever had it, reaching for it and avoiding looking at me, but they were throwing it so fast and everyone was laughing and the sun was bright and I wanted it to stop and—

And—

And—

The hat was in my hands. And then it wasn't. It was on the frozen pond, not even a fifth of the way to the center.

I just wanted it to stop. And the second her hat hit my hands, it had felt as if my skin was burning.

But had I even *held* it? I wasn't sure. There were so many of us, laughing and jumping and reaching. Then Violet's sparkly fingernails. Haddie's bright pink hat. Violet had thrown it, or I had dropped it, or—

Haddie stepped out onto the pond, walking carefully so she wouldn't fall. She was still crying, slowly inching her way across the ice, getting farther from us and closer to the hat.

"Let's go," I said. "You guys, let's *go* . . ."

There was a *crack*, and Haddie fell down hard.

And then, a splash.

Afterward, everyone asked how I knew what to do. I told them it was instinct, or that I'd seen a YouTube video on it. But here's the truth.

Mom has to be constantly on for True U—she calls it "giving off a sense of sparkle." I call it "convincing the person changing the oil on our car that True Transformation Wrinkle-Be-Gone Cream will make her look fifteen years younger." So while Mom pitches Rhonda on how she can save 20 percent by signing up as a True Emerald Beauty Consultant and how she'll make a buttload more money than she currently does wearing a denim jumpsuit and messing with cars, I'm reading every magazine the Jiffy Lube has to offer. I've already made it through *People*, reading about the royal wedding and whether or not the duchess is pregnant. Now I'm on to *Survivalist*, which is breaking down how to save people in life-or-death situations. Avalanches. Forest fires. Thin ice.

Ice, which can look steady and firm, is actually quite fragile. Especially in areas where the weather changes rapidly. One wrong step and it will crack—with a splash, you'll be a goner.

So while Haddie Marks was thrashing around in that pond, her arms flailing, the other kids screaming for help, all I could remember was that magazine. *Survivalist* had told me you should shimmy across the ice on your stomach. So I lay down and started crawling over to her, trying as hard as I could not to put too much weight on any one body part. From the shoreline, I could hear my friends yelling. "Stop, Kate, what are you doing? Stop!" I propped myself up on my forearms and inched forward like a worm. Haddie's face was bopping in and out of the water, with a desperate "Help me! Help me!" each time she broke the surface. I didn't respond, I was so focused. My cheeks felt raw, pressed so close to the ice. I gently stretched an arm out and pressed down, hard, before pulling my body forward, making sure I didn't come across any other thin patches. I made it to the hole where she had fallen, my hand reaching for anything. Before I knew it, her icy fingers grabbed mine. With strength I didn't know I had—Coach Watt would have been proud—I yanked my arm back, hoisting Haddie out of the pond and back onto the ice.

"Do it like me," I huffed out. "On your stomach. Make yourself flat."

It was a warm day, but now I felt so cold—colder than I'd ever been, colder than I could've possibly imagined. The sun was beating down on us, but being pressed against the ice meant that my entire body was starting to go numb. Haddie's long, wet hair was dripping onto my arms. Her lips had a slight blue tinge to them, like Blueberry Jam, a lip gloss color Mom had tried to sell last summer.

She was shivering and crying; her teeth were chattering so hard I was scared they'd break. We shimmied back over the ice together—mostly by me dragging her—to the shore. Someone came running, a boy with a UW Law School sweatshirt on, and he yanked us both up.

"Help is coming," shrieked Taylor, clutching her phone.

"Looks to me like help was already here," said the boy. He was staring at me.

4

I SAT IN THE BACK OF THE AMBULANCE WITH A BLANKET
over my shoulders that smelled like Watson after he
got caught in the rain. I'd told the grumpy paramedic
that I was fine, fine, *fine*, but she insisted I sit there
anyway. Now I was getting grilled by a police officer,
telling the story in as much detail as I could remember.

"Kate. Oh my gosh. Oh my *gosh*."

There he was—Dad. He was off duty, but still drove
up in his copper-mobile, lights blaring. He immediately
started barking at the paramedic in cop-talk. Numbers
and codes and words like *submersion*, *hypothermia*,
frostbite. But then his arms were around me, and even
though it was kind of embarrassing, I buried my face
into his sweatshirt.

"Oh my gosh," he kept repeating, over and over.
"You're freezing."

I wasn't the one who was really hurt. Haddie had

left in an ambulance, zipping off to the hospital. Taylor had disappeared, along with Violet, Amira, Nico, and Brett, so it was just me trying to explain to my dad and the police officer, what had happened on the pond.

"I still don't understand what exactly you kids were doing out there. You said you were just 'hanging out'?" the officer asked.

"Leave her alone, Max," Dad said. "She's exhausted. I'm taking her home." I was surprised he was talking like that. Dad wasn't even thirty, while Max looked pretty close to retirement. Like he'd *seen* some things.

"You're lucky," Max said to me. "You could have been seriously hurt."

"Is Haddie okay?" I asked the paramedic.

"Oh yeah. Don't worry. They'll get her all warmed up at the hospital. That was so brave of you, kid," she said. "Your other friend told me you just crawled right out there. Said she got some video of it happening."

I almost rolled my eyes as I shivered. I didn't even have to ask which friend—of course it was Taylor. When in doubt, take a picture.

"Come on," said Dad. "Let's get you home. You're *sure* you don't want to go get checked out?"

"Positive. I just want to go home."

◆◆◆

You'd think I'd be used to riding in a police car, considering my dad had been a cop since I was four years old, but I still wasn't. The way everyone around you drove so slowly, or the way other drivers glanced through the windows to see who you were. Even though I was in the front seat, most people probably thought I was in trouble, getting carted off to jail.

"So she just *fell through*?" Dad asked. "That's bizarre. What was she doing out on the ice?"

What *was* she doing out on the ice?

The hat. The hat! In all the craziness, in the icy water and the wet-dog-smelling blanket, in the sound of my dad's tires screeching down the street and Taylor's shocked, pale face, I had forgotten why Haddie had been on the pond in the first place.

The hat. The hat that had been in my hands, and then on the ice.

It was an *accident*. Wasn't it?

I had wanted them to *stop*. Hadn't I?

It had all happened so fast. That was how life was with Taylor and her friends. There was hardly time to stop and think.

"We were just . . . hanging out," I answered. "Like I said. And then we looked up, and she was there."

"On the ice?" Dad asked, confused.

"On the ice. Dad, I don't really want to talk about it."

"You're probably beat, huh?" Dad said. "Hey . . . why weren't you at basketball practice?"

"Canceled," I said, leaning my head against the window and shutting my eyes. It seemed like a million years had passed since Mrs. Urbanski had made morning announcements.

Haddie's eyes, looking at me, waiting for me to open my mouth and defend her. Waiting for me to be brave when I wasn't. The memory was burned into my skull. I forced my eyes back open.

"Well, hey. You could have let me *know*, Bird. You're not really supposed to just hang out with friends after school without telling me. Asking me."

"I'm not?" I asked.

"No. Didn't Mom make you call her if plans changed?"

"Um, not really. As long as I didn't do anything stupid."

"Of course she didn't," Dad said with an eye roll. Which made me mad.

Because, no, Mom wasn't perfect. I was the Designated Responsible Person in our apartment who did things like check the ketchup to make sure it hadn't expired and restart the router when the internet wasn't working. But I wished she and Dad would cool it with

44

the hating on each other. Because it can get tiring, hearing about how *Your Father thinks he's all that because he can afford nicer birthday presents* and *Your Mother needs to figure out her finances* and *Your Father didn't feed you french fries for dinner again, did he?* and *Your Mother shouldn't be sleeping past ten, that's ridiculous, she has responsibilities.* As if Your Mother and Your Father were dueling villains instead of my actual mom and dad, who were supposed to be on the same team.

The number one battle they had was over True U. Mom sometimes made choices that were . . . less than smart. I might have been twelve, but come on—even I knew buying a boatload of eye primer to sell instead of getting the dryer fixed was dumb. We'd had to drive to Dad's three times a week with our wet clothes to use his machine. Even though Dad said he didn't care, Mom wouldn't take a loan from him to get it fixed, and they got in a big fight over it, and we wound up having to stay up until midnight drying our jeans with blow dryers. All because of eye primer. What even *is* eye primer? Why would eyes need to be primed, anyway?

And then the argument would be about who was "taking care" of me, like I was a puppy that needed to be let out. Back then, I lived with Mom, but I would go to Dad's house every other weekend. Then I began stopping by during the week sometimes, especially on nights Mom had True U parties at people's homes, because I never knew when she'd get back. Then she started going on trips—a cruise here, a conference there, always put on by True U and always "necessary for work." Sometimes she could bring me, which was super fun, but sometimes she couldn't, so I spent more time at Dad's. Mom wanted that Diamond level so bad, and Aleena, her mentor at True U, kept convincing her that different things would help her get there. If she'd only go to this conference, or buy that promotion package, or, apparently, move to *Utah*. But for a level that was supposed to have her rolling in the dough, it sure felt like she spent a lot of time comparing prices at the grocery store.

They thought they were only complaining about each other, but I was the one who felt it. Because *why* didn't they have normal college degrees? And *why* didn't Mom just have a normal job? And *why* couldn't we live in a normal house, maybe even all together?

Yours truly, that's why.

Maybe not. Maybe Mom was always destined to sell makeup to the neighbors and spend money on bumper stickers instead of nongeneric cereal.

My parents could—and did—tell me how they

wouldn't change a thing, and loved me so much, and were so grateful for God's plan instead of their own. I knew they meant it too. But the fact was, having a kid at sixteen had totally changed their lives. And while some of those changes seemed good (you know, *me*), some of them also seemed kind of hard. And when they complained about what kind of dinners I was eating, about me calling to check in after school, and, most often, about money, I knew they were really complaining about a long string of mistakes. Sometimes, no matter how much I knew it wasn't true, it felt like one of those was me.

"Sorry," I said.

"No, *I'm* sorry," said Dad. "I get it. Different parents, different rules. Must be annoying. But I want to know where you are after school, okay? If it's not in the gym, just text me. And don't forget to say who you're with."

I nodded.

"Hey. I don't know if I said this yet. But I'm really, really proud of you. That was so dangerous, but if you hadn't been out there, I don't know what would have happened to Haddie." Dad grinned at me. "Those were some serious McAllister guts."

I gave him a half smile.

I just wished I could remember how that hat had gotten out of my hands and onto the ice.

♦♦♦

That night, I took the hottest shower I could, trying to let the water scald the memory of that icy pond off me. Then I pulled on my sweats and wolfed down two pieces of the pizza Dad had ordered, before grabbing my phone for some Instagram scrolling while he watched a documentary on the History channel. I spent most of my time in the living room of Dad's apartment. My actual "room" was a sofa bed I felt I was going to fall through at any minute, shoved into a second bedroom that he usually used as an office. The only two things hanging on the walls were a poster of Aaron Rodgers he'd gotten signed a few years ago and the aforementioned painting of Jesus, which was, if I'm being honest, freaky. He was super pale, which He obviously wasn't in real life, and He stared down at me like He knew all my secrets. Dad had promised me we'd redo the room now that I was here "permanently," but I didn't really want to.

It's not permanent, I had reminded him. *Mom's coming back as soon as she makes Diamond.*

Dad had nodded but said that didn't mean we couldn't buy a new bed. I'd still sleep here sometimes, after all.

I scrolled through photo after photo. Taylor and Violet doing a fake laugh in Taylor's room. Maggie, a girl from my science class, with her new puppy. Brett trying to look tough. I clicked over to Haddie's profile, but she hadn't posted anything since a selfie a few days ago. She looked pretty in it, soft and smiling—a *real* smile. She had a heart emoji as the caption. It was weird: you always read in books and saw in movies that popular girls were pretty and geeks who loved anime just . . . weren't. But you couldn't ignore the fact that Haddie was, like, *really* pretty. Way prettier than yours truly, who always felt too tall and could never get all the waves out of my hair no matter how long I spent straightening it. Haddie had olive skin and dark brown hair, with big green eyes that she didn't put makeup on. If she had shopped at Hollister like everyone else, she'd fit in with Taylor's group better than I did. It made me wonder why, exactly, Taylor disliked her so much.

Then I tapped over to a profile that I didn't follow but creeped on regularly.

Casey Whalen, True U Beauty Consultant, True Sapphire. Also known as She Who Abandons People for Utah. Or, Mom.

Photo after photo of her applying lip gloss, waving sample packets of wrinkle cream, and smiling with eyeshadow palettes. Her latest photo was a picture of her and Aleena, arms around each other, smiling huge. I read the caption:

THIS. GIRL. What would I do without her?! 🖤 Aleena is my north ★ in my True U business. I couldn't ask for a better mentor and coach. She's literally letting me crash on her couch so that I can be nearer to headquarters in order to further my #GIRLBOSS career! Everything I do, I do for my family . . . it is SO HARD to be away from my sweet angel Kate but I know that she understands the realities of #momtrepreneur life and that ALL I do is for HER!

As I sat in Dad's apartment, with some old guy on TV talking about Abraham Lincoln's legacy, the smell of pepperoni filling the air, and Watson scratching at the door to be let out, I stared at my mom, #girlbossing her way to Diamond level in La La Lip Gloss Land and convincing her two thousand followers that everything she did was for me.

I wondered if I could convince myself. Maybe it was true. Maybe Mom really would hit True Diamond level and become one of those consultants like Aleena who gets to just encourage other people on her team and doesn't have to buy that much makeup herself. Maybe she'd take me on her next True U cruise, when the

Diamonds get recognized, and she'd be given that small diamond heart necklace that top consultants get, as the rest of the group bursts into cheers, looking up to her like a role model. We'd win a True Tesla, the car Diamonds drove around, and we'd ride off into the sunset.

The photo of my mom and Aleena suddenly disappeared and was replaced by a snapshot of me and Taylor. She was calling me. I answered quickly.

"Hey," I said.

"Oh my God!" she shrieked. "Turn on the news! Channel 6! Right now!"

"Dad," I asked, "can we switch it to the news quick?"

"Why?" he asked, his eyes not leaving a graphic of Lincoln giving the Gettysburg Address.

"Why?" I asked Taylor.

"Just do it!"

"I don't know," I told him. "Just for a sec. Channel 6."

He reached over for the remote and flicked to Channel 6. There was a grainy cell phone video of—

A bright purple jacket.

Me.

Me and Haddie, to be more precise. Me slithering across the pond like a snake, my arms reaching for her. Me tugging her out of the ice—man, I looked ridiculous—and the two of us crawling back to shore. Our faces were blurred.

"Wait . . . is that *you*?" asked Dad. But he didn't sound happy. He sounded *furious*.

"What the heck?" I asked Taylor.

"I sent them the video!" she shrieked. "They were so into it. They called and asked my dad if they could play it—wait for it, I think they're about to play the part with my voice . . ."

And there it was.

"It was *so* scary," said TV Taylor. "But my *best* friend was just super, super brave—"

"They wouldn't let me say your name!" said Phone Taylor. "And I couldn't give them your phone number to contact you because your dad is such a psycho."

I winced. Taylor could always get away with saying things so much harsher than anyone else. She *was* right, though. Since he was a cop, my dad was hyper-aware of who had our phone numbers and address. I guess when people are in jail because of you, you don't exactly want to risk them trying to get in touch with you or your twelve-year-old.

TV Taylor kept chattering. "I know everyone's so worried about bullies, but like, me and my friends try hard to be the kind ones, you know? We always want to look out for other people."

"How good do I sound?" squealed Phone Taylor.

"Geez! Thank God they blurred your face. It's outrageous that they didn't get my permission to show this," said Dad, fuming.

"Shh," I said. "Both of you! I can't hear."

The camera flashed from the footage of the rescue to the newscaster, a woman with long hair and a serious expression.

"I must say—in a world where the bullying epidemic rages on, it's nice to know that there are kids out there taking care of each other. This has been Bao Nguyen, reporting for Channel 6."

I told Taylor I had to go.

"You're welcome," she chirped cheerfully—the second time she'd said it today without me having thanked her.

The TV switched to a commercial for cat food, and Dad shook his head angrily.

"They shouldn't be able to show any part of you on television without getting my permission," he said.

"Dad. *Chill*. It's not like anyone could even tell it was me. And they didn't use my name."

He looked at me. "I know you think I'm a little overprotective, Kate."

"A *little*? I can't even use my name on Instagram."

I was Katherine Louise, my middle name, not Kate McAllister.

"You're lucky you're allowed to have one of those at all. When you see the things I see every single day, you know that the world can be a scary place. It may seem fun to draw attention to yourself, and I know you kids these days all want to be internet celebrities with YouTube channels—"

"Dad." I gave him a look. I hated when he got all *kids these days*, especially because, hello, it wasn't like he was a caveman. "Have you ever seen me attempt to make a YouTube video?"

"No! I'm just *saying*. You know what I had to do yesterday? Go talk to a high school boy who wouldn't stop texting his ex-girlfriend eighty times a day. He keyed her car. He knows where she lives . . . We're lucky she told her mom, who called us. Angry people are *dangerous*. You need to protect yourself."

"Okay! *Okay*. I didn't send the video in, Dad. It had nothing to do with me. I would never do something like that."

"I know," he said, sighing. "You have a better head on your shoulders than those girls you've been hanging out with this year. I know that." He leaned over and kissed the top of my head. "I'm gonna call it an early night. You have homework?"

"I was maybe going to call Mom," I said.

"Okay. Let me talk if you get through, okay? I tried to call her earlier, but she didn't answer."

"Will do."

Dad ducked into his room and I called Mom, her phone ringing a few times before she answered.

"Katie lady, do you need something?" she whispered. "I'm at a party." She didn't mean a *fun* party, one with games and dancing. She meant a party at someone's house, where she gave makeovers and tried to convince people to sign up as True Emeralds, the lowest rung on the True U ladder. "Aleena set it all up for me. You know what I always say: True Girl Bosses never rest."

I heard someone laugh in the background. "It's just . . . well, I had kind of a bad day."

"You did? Oh man. Well . . . hold on a minute." There was some muffled talking, then silence. Mom came back. "Okay, I went into the bathroom for a sec. What happened?"

I told her the entire story of Haddie falling through the ice. Well, not the *entire* story. I kind of left out the fact that the hat had maybe been in my hands before it was on the ice. Or that we'd been making fun of

Haddie. Or that Brett had been there—Mom had met him once and totally hated him.

"Wow. I'm so proud of you! You must have been terrified. But of course, you let your *courage* be your *compass*." Another True U–ism.

"There was even a clip from Taylor's phone that they played on the local news," I said. I was about to tell her how Dad had freaked out, but stopped when I heard someone else talking in the background on Mom's end.

"Oops—can I call you tomorrow, Katie lady? Someone here has a few questions about our True U consultant discount."

"Yeah. Sure. I love you."

"Love you too," she said before hanging up.

I just stared at my phone, realizing I hadn't even had time to give the phone to Dad like he'd asked. Mom seemed to be getting busier and busier, even though I got the feeling her business wasn't going super well. Last year, if Haddie had been bugging me or I'd had a crappy basketball practice, Mom and I would have made massive ice cream sundaes and talked over every little detail while some wedding dress shopping show played in the background.

I suddenly remembered a trip we went on last summer, only a week before Haddie and I caught those fireflies. Mom had won some random bonus for signing up a ton of True Emeralds, but it wasn't big enough for a plane ticket anywhere. Instead, we got in the car and drove north—toward the Northwoods of Wisconsin, where she and her own mom had gone on a rare vacation once, staying at a cabin and eating s'mores.

After hours of driving, when it was almost midnight, we found a resort in a little town called Moose Junction and checked into one of their cabins. As we were dragging our duffel bags in, Mom grabbed my arm.

"Kate. Stop. Look," she said excitedly.

"Look at what?" I was being bitten by mosquitos and there was a major chill in the air. I wanted to get inside and crawl under the covers.

She gestured up to the sky. It was pitch-black but covered with the most spectacular array of stars I'd ever seen. They were sprinkled above us like diamonds, glowing and winking.

"Like a map," she whispered. "To wherever we want to go, right? Our very own spotlights."

That weekend was one of the best I'd ever had. We ate ice cream at almost every meal, jumped in the lake instead of showering, and stayed up late watching rom-coms. Her pumping me for gossip about boys I had crushes on. Me laughing and denying it all.

Sitting there in Dad's apartment, I missed her so badly, I thought I might cry. That Instagram post—she had said she was doing everything for *me*. But what if the only thing I wanted was for her to come back?

5

THE NEXT MORNING, DAD GRABBED THE REMOTE AND TURNED on the news as I poured myself orange juice.

"I got the fancy stuff you like," Dad said. "The kind with pulp."

I didn't respond. I probably should have said thank you. But I was kind of annoyed about the night before. I'd saved Haddie's life, and all he could focus on was why I shouldn't be on TV.

I was also worried about what was going to happen at school. Would the whole thing make life easier on Haddie? Or harder? Would her almost dying make Taylor and the rest of our crew leave her alone? Or would they come up with a new way to torment her?

I pulled up YouTube on my phone. My favorite vlogger, Cory Seymour, had posted a new video. He used to have a TV show, but then he got in trouble for setting his car on fire in the middle of the street. He was always pulling these goofy pranks, and he invited other YouTube celebrities to live in this giant California mansion with him. Sometimes he interviewed people who had done what he called "legit inspiring stuff." But I liked the prank episodes best. Like the one where he turned every single thing in his friend's bedroom upside down and then filmed the guy's reaction. Haddie and I used to spend hours binge-watching Cory Seymour episodes we'd seen a million times. Taylor and her crew loved him too—practically everyone at our school was a Cory Seymour megafan.

The closing segment of *Wake Up Wisconsin* started blaring from the TV, yanking my attention away from my phone.

"And before we go today, we want to show you a quick clip that should brighten up your Thursday," said a white newscaster with brown hair. He looked like the kind of guy you see in a toothpaste commercial: a shiny smile and perfect hair. "Let's roll it."

I dropped my phone and almost spat out my orange juice. There was . . . *me*. Pulling Haddie out of the lake.

My face in full view.

Dad and I both froze. This clip was different from the one on Channel 6. Well, it was the same clip. But it was so obviously me. And along the bottom of the screen in bold letters it said: *Madison Middle Schooler Saves the Day*.

"In the midst of the bullying epidemic, which we discussed here on *Wake Up Wisconsin* just last week, it's so refreshing to see a young girl willing to risk it all for her classmate and save the day. Katherine McAllister is a seventh grader at East Middle School, where she's a member of the basketball team and spends her spare time, apparently, saving lives. We have her mother on the line. Mrs. McAllister, where did your daughter get her bravery from?"

"Well, Kyle, it's actually Miss Whalen, but you can call me Casey," said Mom.

I looked at my dad. He was still frozen, simply staring at the TV. Even Watson could tell there was something wrong. He sat at full attention, not even barking for an extra helping of food in his little bowl like he normally did. I couldn't believe Dad wasn't yelling or screaming or lunging for the phone to call Mom.

"Kate's always been such a brave girl," she continued, answering the newscaster's question. "I'd like to think that part of it comes from me, as someone who works to help women step into their own spotlight as a True U Beauty Consultant. And I'm sure part of it comes from her dad as well. He's a police officer."

"That was nice of her," I said meekly, but Dad just threw a hand up, as in, *Shut up, Kate*. He didn't take his eyes away from the TV.

"Where did she learn how to properly rescue someone who's fallen through ice?" the anchor asked. "We spoke to the fire chief in Madison and he said that her technique was spot-on."

"That, I'm not sure of. But I know this about Kate: she'll do anything for anyone. You hear about girls at that age being mean to each other, but Kate's always wanted to rise by lifting others." Another True U-ism.

"Well, Miss Whalen, you should be mighty proud. I think all middle schoolers today could take a page out of Kate's book. Now, on to Shelby Davis with the weather."

The camera switched to a redheaded woman waving her arm around a map and saying words like *wintery slush mix*, which nobody wants to hear. Dad hadn't moved a muscle.

"Dad?" I asked, practically whispering.

He blinked. "Kate. Could you please call a friend and see if you can find a different ride to school?"

"Um, sure."

We still didn't move. Dad stared at Shelby Davis so hard, I thought he might break the TV. It reminded me of *Matilda*, when the little girl concentrates to put Cheerios on a spoon with her mind.

"Are you . . . are you going to work?"

"Yes. I am." Dad used to work more nights and weekends and random times, but when he found out I was moving in, he talked to the chief about his schedule, and now he has more regular hours. "But first . . . first, I am going to call your mother."

I nodded. "You know I didn't tell her to do that, right?"

"I know. Please call one of the basketball girls or something."

I took that *or something* as permission to ask Taylor instead, even though Dad probably wasn't her number one fan at the moment. I quickly texted her and told her I had spent the night at my dad's, and could she please-please-please pick me up so I wouldn't have to ride to school in a cop car yet again? As soon as the Tobitts' familiar silver Subaru pulled up in front of Dad's building, I took off out the door and down the stairs. I practically ran into Mrs. Levine, who lived next door and spent most of her time knitting blankets for her grandkids and reporting the neighbors to my dad for playing their music too loudly.

"I saw you on *Wake Up Wisconsin*, Kate!" she said excitedly. "You're a real celebrity now."

"Not quite, Mrs. Levine," I said.

"Our very own Greta Garbo."

"Who?"

"Never mind. Old film star. You kids need a little more culture in your lives."

"Noted."

"You have a good day at school, now."

I burst out the front door and got into the Subaru, where Taylor was holding her wet nails out in front of her.

"Watch the slam," said Stephanie, wincing as I shut the car door.

"Sorry," I said. "Thanks for the ride." Stephanie was Taylor's Not-Mom. I didn't know how else to describe her. She was nice enough in that way where you feel like someone is constantly annoyed by you but is trying to put on a happy face. The first time I went over to Taylor's, Stephanie had just made an entire batch of kale-spirulina brownies, which were . . . about as delicious as they sounded.

"That was nice of your mom," I'd said, biting into one and instantly regretting it.

"She's not my mom," Taylor had replied flatly. "She's my dad's girlfriend."

Well, I knew all about the awkwardness of that.

My parents had dated plenty of people, and while I could remember a few by the things they'd been around for—Dad had been seeing Lana when I got my braces off, Mom had been going on dates with Mario when she joined True U—neither of them really liked to introduce me to someone until it was "serious." Which it rarely became. I couldn't imagine someone moving *in*.

"Where's your mom?" I had asked Taylor.

"Paris," she'd said. "She works in fashion." Of course she did. Taylor Tobitt had the most glamorous everything, from her clothes to her makeup to her mother, apparently. My mom sold lipstick to the neighbors. Taylor's mom probably designed dresses for actresses to wear on red carpets.

But Taylor didn't seem too happy about it, so I never brought it up again. It could have been something we talked about, I guess—something we had in common. Moms who ditched us. But that wasn't the kind of thing Taylor and I really . . . bonded over. Hard stuff about my mom—that's the kind of thing I used to share with Haddie. I just liked knowing that Taylor *got it*, in a way Haddie never would.

But that still didn't mean I was telling Taylor about my move.

"Stephanie," Taylor said, her voice dripping sugary-sweet. "What do you say to a lunch drop-off?" Occasionally, Stephanie would bring us fast food for lunch and we'd pick it up in the office. I loved when she did that. Because the food was good, yeah, but more because everyone saw Taylor and me eating the same noncafeteria lunches and knew we were best friends.

"I say . . . sure. Noodles and Company?"

"Two mac and cheeses, with a Rice Krispies Treat to split? You're the best," said Taylor. She wiggled her eyebrows at me happily. I grinned. It was a perk of Taylor friendship: that the normal, everyday things like lunch could be made special.

"Thanks, Stephanie," I said.

"Anything for our local hero," she replied, smiling at me in the rearview mirror.

"Yeah," said Taylor, "Violet texted that your mom was on *Wake Up Wisconsin* this morning! She said they showed your face and name and everything."

"I guess Mom gave them permission. I don't really know," I admitted.

"Well, I think it's awesome," said Taylor, nudging me with her knee. "I already knew you were totally kick-butt. Now the rest of the world does too."

"Why did you even send it to them?" I asked.

She laughed. "I don't know. Because I had it. And

you seemed kinda down yesterday. Lately, in fact."

"What do you mean?"

"I don't know. Just . . . like, for the past few weeks or whatever, you haven't laughed as much. I thought maybe something was bugging you."

"What makes you think that?" I asked.

"Girl. Yesterday at lunch Amira did her Mr. Kim impression, and you didn't even crack a smile."

Taylor could notice things when she wanted to. Care, even. Maybe she *was* someone I could be my real self around. Maybe she *was* the kind of friend I could call when my life was falling apart. Maybe—

Stephanie slammed on the brakes as a minivan cut us off. She laid on the horn and yelled a swear word out the window. Taylor rolled her eyes at me, grinning.

"You're my best friend," she said, "and I thought you could use some people cheering you on."

It was one of those rare moments that reminded me why I had sat at her lunch table in the first place—when I caught Taylor's sunshine poking through her tough-girl clouds and saw, for a glimpse, the real girl underneath.

All day long, things got weirder and weirder.

In homeroom, Haddie never showed. I hoped she was okay. Her face had still been blurred out on the news segment, so apparently her parents hadn't given any kind of permission. I was kind of grateful. The last thing we needed was for the whole story to come out and for East Middle School to be the latest bull's-eye on the bullying target.

During second period, I got called into the principal's office. I didn't mind missing math—all those numbers and shapes gave me a headache. I never wanted to be the kid who asked a million questions, but if I didn't, the class got way too far ahead of me. So I gladly took the note from the student aide and headed down the hall. But at the same time, I was nervous. I'd never been called into Principal Howe's office in my life. I didn't even think she knew my name.

"Kate McAllister! Come in, come in." Principal Howe looked up from what she had been typing and gestured toward the soft orange chair across from her desk. I slid into the seat and looked around. Her office was completely covered with inspirational animal posters, like dolphins reminding us to *Dream Big* and kittens somehow trying to evoke the idea that *Kindness Comes First*. They were like True U posters gone wrong.

"Hi," I said.

"Hello, hello," she replied. "Sorry to pull you out of second period."

"Pre-algebra," I said. "Not exactly my favorite, so . . ."

She smiled. "I wanted to ask you about what happened yesterday at the pond. Do you mind filling me in?"

"Um." I swallowed.

The hat.

My hands.

The pond.

Splash.

Through it all, Haddie's eyes meeting mine. A thousand sleepovers, six birthday parties, a camping trip Dad had dragged me on where it rained the entire time and we spent all night playing Apples to Apples in the tent.

What happened?

"Haddie Marks fell through the ice," I said. "I remembered reading an article once. About how to save someone who did that. And . . . I don't know. Instincts, I guess? Like how regular people can lift up cars in accidents and stuff?"

"Very impressive," said Principal Howe, raising an eyebrow. "And you were the only one there?"

"No. Taylor Tobitt. And Violet Marrigan, Amira Razak. Brett Browning, Nico St. George."

"Why was Haddie on the ice in the first place?"

Because of me. Maybe.

"I don't know," I said.

"Well, whatever the case, I'm certainly glad she's all right. And I'm honored that an East Middle School Knight had the bravery to do such a thing. You likely saved her life."

Wait—I *did*, didn't I?

What if I hadn't been there?

The thought of Haddie, the same Haddie I knew better than anyone else, just not being here . . .

What if I'd never opened that magazine? What if Haddie was *dead* right now? It happened every day—kids dying from car crashes or cancer or drowning in freezing pond water. That could have really, truly happened. It hadn't really hit me until right then. I felt like I was going to cry.

"I have some exciting news. *The Morning Buzz* called," she said, snapping me back to the moment. "Are you familiar?"

Of course I was. It seemed like everyone in the world tuned into *The Morning Buzz*. I followed Maria Ramirez, one of their anchors, on Instagram. She was always sharing cute videos of her puppy.

"Yeah," I said. "Why did they call?"

"They want to do a special!" she said excitedly, clapping her hands together. "Send cameras to the school.

Talk to you and Haddie. They said a feel-good story is just what our world needs right now."

The Morning Buzz? Me and Haddie? On national news? It was all so much, so fast. A whirlwind of new things, smacking me in the face: switching lunch tables, moving in with Dad . . . now being the poster girl of a movement I really didn't belong to? Weren't there way nicer kids they should be spotlighting instead of me, just someone who happened to read a magazine in a Jiffy Lube waiting room?

"Principal Howe . . . I don't know. Is Haddie even okay? She isn't in school today. And my dad . . . He can be kind of weird about this stuff. He wasn't happy my mom gave *Wake Up Wisconsin* permission to show me . . ." A look of surprise flickered across Principal Howe's face and I shut my mouth up real fast. I hated spilling my parents' personal business to people who didn't need to know.

Principal Howe nodded, her eyes softening. "Yes. I totally understand. Well, for the record, Haddie is completely fine. She just needed a day to recuperate from the craziness, but she didn't even have to spend the night in the hospital. I spoke to her mother this morning, and she said she actually wanted to call you tonight to thank you personally."

I almost winced. Haddie's mom, Juliet, had always been so nice to me. How was I supposed to explain why I hadn't been around all year?

"And as for your dad, the producer told me he's planning on calling him later this morning. They needed to speak to me to see if they could do some filming at school—show the lunchroom, maybe interview a handful of kids. Why don't you speak with your dad tonight, and I'll give him a call as well? I'm sure he'd understand the importance of your bravery inspiring other middle schoolers around the country," she assured me. "We actually have your mother as the main contact for you on file. Is that . . . should that be changed? Are you currently with your father?"

"Um," I said, "it's temporary. Keep my mom on file. But call my dad. If you don't have the number, he works at the police station on Bluemound Road, and they can connect you. But I'll talk to him tonight."

"Great," she said. "Keep me posted. I think it's time the world got to see the real East Middle School."

I HAD NEVER THOUGHT OF MYSELF AS A VERY SPORTY PERSON. I mean, I did hit a home run in T-ball once, but that was because Dawn Grahn was making a bracelet out of daisies in the outfield and didn't notice the ball go sailing past her. My hand-eye coordination is lacking, to say the least. But I'm on the basketball team for one reason and one reason only.

I'm tall.

The very first week of sixth grade, Coach Watt came up to me in the hallway. She was also our sixth-grade civics teacher, but it was no secret that her true obsession was the basketball team. Her entire classroom was covered in Wisconsin Badgers posters.

"How tall are you?" she asked. Just like that. I was tempted to spit back, *What's your weight? How many gray hairs do you have?*

"Five nine," I said. Which, I mean, was it a lie? Not

technically. The last time I'd been measured I was five nine. But that had been at my yearly doctor's appointment five months before, and I'd definitely grown since then.

Her eyes lit up. "You play ball?"

"As in . . . basketball?"

"Yes!"

"No," I said. "I mean, the YMCA in first grade . . ."

She waved a hand. "Doesn't matter. A girl your height belongs on our team. Tryouts are next Tuesday after school."

"I really don't . . ."

"See you there!"

Coach Watt wasn't great at taking no for an answer.

And so that's how I found myself in the gym the following week. I only knew a third of the girls; everyone else had come from the other elementary school that funneled into East for junior high.

Coach Watt stood up in front of everyone and went on and on about trying your best and hustling your heart out. Her arms were so muscly she looked like she could knock your teeth out, and she kept her honey-blond hair in a tight ponytail. It almost sounded like she was giving one of the speeches my mom recited on her monthly team Skype calls to the True U Emeralds.

"The only thing standing between you and the player you want to be is your work ethic," Coach Watt said. Now, I was *positive* I'd read that in a True U Entrepren-U-ership pamphlet.

We started with layups, and I could see Coach Watt's face slowly falling. I missed almost every shot. I mean, I was genuinely terrible. I had warned her.

"Kate," she asked me about halfway through, "are you maybe left-handed? And just . . . never knew it?"

"Doubtful," I said. I tried a left-handed layup and it went flying into the bleachers.

Luckily, a few other girls were super good, so she quickly moved on from me while I stood there wondering if there were any sports that didn't require hand-eye coordination. During the last half hour of tryouts, we set up for a scrimmage.

Coach Watt had switched focus to girls who could actually get the ball kinda-sorta close-ish to the hoop. It was kind of a relief to not feel her eyes staring me down during every single drill. Dawn Grahn had apparently retired from a life of natural jewelry during our T-ball days and become a superstar athlete, because she was easily the best girl at tryouts. She shot a midrange jumper and it bounced off the rim. I leaped up and grabbed it, then threw it back to her.

She shot again, missed again. I grabbed the ball a second time and tossed it back to her.

Swish.

"Good work, Kate," said Coach, even though Dawn was the one who'd made the shot. She gave me a high five and we jogged to the other end of the court. A tall girl with cornrows shot and missed, and I leaped up again to grab the ball. Back to Dawn. She darted across the court like a rocket and made another basket.

And my fate was sealed.

So, I can't shoot for crap. But I have two roles on the East Middle School basketball team. The first, according to Coach, is to psych the other team out and get them to double-guard me until they realize I'm, well, not the best shooter on the court. The second is to rebound. Over and over and over again.

That means after school, from November to March, I'm in a sweaty gym grabbing balls and tossing them to Dawn or Houa or Alex or Nikki. And to be honest, I like that job. There's a lot less pressure. I don't have to aim the ball perfectly, getting it to fly through the hoop. I just have to leap in the air and snatch it. There's something comforting about the gym, whether it's the sound of squeaking tennis shoes or the smell of rubber in the air. Or maybe it's just that feeling of being part of a team—a team that isn't going to kick you out if you say the wrong thing or miss a basket.

Today, like every other single practice, we were starting with a rainbow drill. You line up in an arc and take turns shooting and rebounding. It was a nice way to warm up our muscles without having to sweat our faces off.

"Dude, I saw you on TV this morning!" said Houa excitedly as she got into line behind me. She called everyone *dude*.

"Me too," said Shayla, tightening her ponytail. "Haddie wasn't in math today. Think she's okay?"

"Yeah," I said awkwardly. "Principal Howe said she was doing good."

"Why'd you get called into her office, anyway?" asked Houa.

"Girls! Look alive!" barked Coach Watt. Nikki had just made a layup and I hadn't run forward to rebound it.

"Sorry," I said, jogging toward the ball. I grabbed it and passed it to Dawn, on the other end, before regaining my place in line. Houa rebounded Dawn's ball and was behind me in line again.

"She said *The Morning Buzz* wants to come do a segment," I told her.

"On *you*?" she asked.

"I guess? I think just on, like, kids being nice to each other."

"That's so cool!"

I didn't say what I was thinking, which was that there was no way on earth Dad was going to let me be interviewed on national TV, or that I felt like this whole thing was getting out of hand. One segment on a local morning show was one thing. But *The Morning Buzz*?

"Well, I saw that clip, like, all over Instagram," said Shayla, jogging to join our line behind Houa after rebounding Alex's miss. "*People* shared it. Right after a story about Ariana Grande's new boyfriend."

"You're, like, a rock star," said Dawn.

"*Girls*. This isn't lunchtime. We're supposed to be preparing for game 3 of the championships, and we already had to miss a practice this week. Focus," said Coach Watt. "We can all go goo-goo gaga over our hometown celebrity later."

My face grew hot and everyone laughed.

After two hours of shooting drills, running laps, and a scrimmage where I actually scored a basket—maybe saving someone's life was bringing me good karma, after all—practice was finally over. I felt like a huge ball of sweat.

"Hey, anyone want to sleep over Saturday night?"

asked Shayla as we all changed back into our street shoes. "We could stream the new *Captain Marvel* movie."

"I'll ask my mom, but that sounds awesome," said Houa. Alex and Dawn said the same thing.

"Kate?" Shayla asked.

"Maybe," I said. I hadn't talked to Taylor about our plans for the weekend. I saw Shayla and Dawn catch each other's eyes and felt my face turn red again.

I liked the girls on the team. A lot. They were fun, and I liked spending time with them, shooting hoops and winning games. But basketball took up a lot of my time, so I didn't always hang out with them outside of it. Besides, I didn't want to make Taylor mad. If I said no to a sleepover *she* invited me to, I never knew if I'd be invited back to another one. It bugged Taylor, the idea of me getting invited anywhere by anyone but her. It's not like I was Miss Popular. But whenever I went to team dinners or whatever, she'd make a joke about it later, how she was so glad I found a group of people who loved how tall I was.

Mean, but what was I supposed to say? See? It was harder than it sounded, being friends with Taylor.

It was exhausting, to be honest: harder than basketball practice. Harder than being Haddie's friend had ever been. It was like I was constantly auditioning for something, but never quite landing the role. I always had to have my guard up with Taylor, like not making weekend plans without knowing what she had in mind, or not quite being able to guess if a joke I made was going to get a laugh, an eye roll, or an icy glare. But I knew I would never fully be able to relax, no matter how long I kept up the act. Taylor had been friends with Violet since first grade, and she could still hand Violet the camera instead of inviting her to be in the photo, or make fun of the way Violet had a bulky hand-me-down backpack instead of a cool messenger bag like most of the other girls. It wasn't going to get easier.

The basketball team was nice. They were funny and helpful, and I didn't feel like I was performing. But that was in the gym. During school, they barely even said hi to me in the hallways, and I did the same. They thought Taylor, Violet, and Amira were stuck-up. Taylor thought they were babyish, the way they'd rather shoot hoops on weekends than make TikToks. And most of the time, I *liked* knowing that I had places to be on the weekend—that I wouldn't be just sitting at home, but with friends, and we'd have something to laugh about at school on Monday. I could change houses and parents and lives, but I would usually be at Taylor's on Saturday night, and that steadiness

80

meant something to me.

But sometimes, I'd glance at the lunch table where the basketball girls were and wish I could sit there for a few minutes instead.

Dad had arranged for Dawn's stepmom to drive me home from basketball, but as we left the gym, I was surprised to see him in the parking lot, leaning against his cop car. I groaned—not another ride in the copper-mobile. He waved a hand in the air and I hurried over, avoiding eye contact with anyone else. Plus, I was kind of ticked at Shayla and Dawn for the look they had shared about my response to the sleepover.

"Hey," I said. "What are you doing here?"

"I want to chat," he said. "Hop in. I thought we could go get OHOP."

OHOP was kind of me and my dad's place. In elementary school, when I'd had a weekly Wednesday-night dinner with him—before I started spending less time at Mom's True U parties and more time at his apartment— we always went to OHOP. It didn't matter that it was dinnertime, or that I always ordered chocolate chip pancakes with chocolate whipped cream. Luna, the owner, knew her way around a griddle. But she wasn't the most *creative* at naming restaurants. Hence the Original House of Pancakes.

"Heck yeah," I said, dropping my backpack by my feet. "I'm starving. I could use some real food."

Dad flicked my knee. "Hey, now. Is my cooking that bad?"

"Well," I said as we pulled out, "no. I just . . . could go for something other than pizza."

Dad winced. "Sorry. I'm not used to having to feed another human regularly. Watson doesn't complain about a nightly meal of kibble and pizza crusts."

"I cooked for me and Mom a lot. I can make dinner once in a while," I said.

"You did?" he asked, surprised.

"I mean, nothing *fancy*. But I can bake a chicken."

"All right, Bobby Flay. You give me a grocery list; I'll buy whatever you need."

I stared out the window as we turned onto the street from the parking lot. "Catch any bad guys today?" I used to think it was so cool that Dad was a cop—out there keeping the streets safe and sometimes coming to pick me up in his uniform. I used to ask him that same question every time I saw him. I thought he was a superhero like Batman, but *real*. Now that I was in middle school, it was usually more embarrassing than interesting. But I still liked hearing about his days.

He rolled his eyes. "A chair theft."

"A *what*? Don't tell me—the terrace chairs." The terrace at the University of Wisconsin was basically the college's huge back porch, where people went to study, drink beer, or listen to music. During the warmer months, it was filled with families getting ice cream and feeding the too-friendly ducks. It had these famous chairs with sunburst patterns in orange, green, and yellow. What made them special was that they were a symbol of Madison, but you couldn't buy them anywhere. Even if you offered a thousand bucks—nope, nada, no sale. You could buy them in the UW colors, red or white, sure, but not the *official* chairs. So people were always trying to steal them.

"Like, in the back of your pickup truck? At least try to be sneaky," he said.

"Sounds like a boring day."

"When you're a cop, boring days are your best days," he reminded me.

We got to OHOP and settled into a corner booth. The top of the table was slightly sticky from someone else's syrup, and the laminated menus were covered in pictures.

"What'll y'all have?" drawled our waitress, a girl about Dad's age with an accent that sounded like she lived in Alabama instead of Wisconsin.

"I'll do a short stack. Bacon on the side. Make it extra crispy, please," he said.

"Sure thing, sweetie." She tried to say it all friendly-like, but I saw the way she was looking at my dad. Let's just say women . . . talked to him a lot. A *lot*. Something about that ugly blue polyester uniform and the fact that he looked like he could still be in college. Like, hello. He's sitting with his *kid*.

"Chocolate chip," I said, interrupting her googly eyes. "And a Diet Coke."

"Got it. Be back in just a jiff," she said, taking our menus and hurrying away.

"You shouldn't be drinking that crap," Dad told me.

"Bacon's worse for you than Diet Coke!"

"Really? No way," Dad said. "At least it's real food."

"I need caffeine," I said.

"Exhausted from all of your heroic activities? Did you, like, pull someone from a fire today?"

"*No.* Coach made us run laps at the end of practice, and I feel like my legs are going to fall off. Thanks for picking me up, though."

Dad cleared his throat. "Right. About that."

Here it came.

"I talked to your mom," he said. "I expressed my disappointment. I know you two think I'm dramatic or whatever about personal details, but again, when you've seen what I've seen . . ."

I rolled my eyes. "Dad. Don't go all old-man cop on me."

"I'm just saying!" He raised his hands in the air. "I'm just *saying*. Your privacy is important to me. I'm your dad and that's my job. But what's done is done. But I wanted to talk to you, actually. About Mom."

"What about her?" I said.

Dad's phone beeped, and he glanced at it quickly before groaning. "Actually, one more thing. This guy from *The Morning Buzz* keeps emailing me. He wants to do, like, an antibullying thing with you and Haddie."

"Principal Howe told me," I said. "She said they asked if they could film at school."

"Do you *want* to do this?" he said. "I mean, think about it. The whole world seeing your face? Someone dumb could go online and, like, make fun of your hair or something. You know how trolls are."

"Like I care," I said. "Geez. I'm not that shallow." Well—sometimes. I'd rather have a random stranger comment on my hair than Taylor.

"I *know*. Don't bite my head off. Let me think about it. I'll talk to Principal Howe tonight."

"You like Maria Ramirez," I reminded him.

He laughed. "I do. Maybe you can get me a date." I threw a jelly packet at him, and he ducked and laughed.

I got up to go to the bathroom, and when I got back, our waitress was delivering the food. She was leaning over, laughing too loudly at something Dad had said, and he was smiling. And something about it made me feel small. I don't know what. But seeing him, how he could have been, young and eating pancakes and flirting with a waitress, instead of having to take care of me, it just made me feel—

Not as tall as I was.

7

AS WE DROVE HOME, I REMEMBERED THAT DAD HAD BEEN about to tell me something about Mom. But when I asked, he just looked distracted.

"Oh yeah. When I was talking to her, she said . . . she said she misses you. That's all."

"*That's* what you had to tell me?" I asked, confused, as we turned off the main road, toward our apartment.

"Yeah. Wait, aren't those your friends?"

There they were: Taylor and Violet, walking together past Ella's Deli, giggling about something. It was already starting to get dark out, but I could still see them—looking at something on Violet's phone. It was cold again; Taylor's breath formed a puff of mist as she laughed. A thousand thoughts burst into my head like fireworks: *Why didn't they call me? Why do I even care—I had fun with Dad! What are they looking at? Are they laughing at something about me? Should I say hi? Should I duck?*

But before I could even say *yeah*, Dad honked his horn, one short beep. The girls jumped, and when they saw me, they smiled and waved. I waved back, all thoughts of Mom flying out the window.

That night, as Dad was in his room on the phone with Principal Howe, I stared at my own phone. I knew what I had to do, but I had absolutely no desire to do it. I would rather have dived back into the icy pond, or given Watson a bath, or sat through a True U presentation with my mom on being a True-ly Authentic Girl Boss.

But I had to call Haddie.

I'd called her so many times before. For practically my entire life, she'd been the person I'd go to with good news or bad news or nothing news, just an invitation to hang out. So why was I so petrified of calling her now?

Um, maybe because I'd treated her like crap all year?

Watson sat blinking at me.

You saved her life, his eyes seemed to say.

I was maybe the reason she risked it in the first place, I thought.

She might not even know that, Watson said. Wait, what? He was a dog. He couldn't *say* anything. Why was I talking to a dog?

I shook my head as if my thoughts could be erased like an Etch A Sketch. I went to my contacts and hit Haddie's number.

As it rang, I wondered if I should just hang up. Let the whole hat thing fade away, sinking to the bottom of the pond. Maybe we could pretend this never happened. Maybe—

"Hello?"

"Hey," I said. "It's . . . it's me." Which, *dumb*. She could see it was me calling.

"Mom, it's Kate. Shh," I heard her say, and the chatter in the background fell a bit. "Kate. Hi."

"I wanted to see how you were doing," I said. "Make sure you were okay."

"I'm okay. I think. I wasn't even underwater for that long. People are being kind of dramatic about it." She laughed, but not a *real* laugh. Not the kind she'd laugh after midnight at a sleepover when we were sugar-drunk off Pixy Stix and watching YouTube videos of kittens dancing.

"Yeah. But still. Scary," I said.

"Super scary," she said.

We sat there, in that uncomfortable silence. It was *Haddie*, my best friend. The person I could tell any-thing to. But it was like we'd never even known each other. Like I hadn't written her a note every single day in fifth grade, folding them into different shapes each time. That jar of fireflies felt so long ago.

"I guess I should say thank you," she said. "You know. For saving my life."

"You don't have to do that," I mumbled.

"No. I do. I mean, if Taylor and Brett hadn't been idiots and thrown my hat . . . I shouldn't have gone out there either. So dumb. Whatever. You could have really gotten hurt. We could have died, the nurse at UW said. So thanks."

If Taylor and Brett—

"Yeah," I heard myself saying. "Well, I'm just really glad you're okay."

"Hey, did Principal Howe talk to you about *The Morning Buzz* thing?"

"She did," I said, surprised, but I guess I shouldn't have been. Duh, they'd want to talk to the girl whose life got saved.

"My mom didn't really want my name out there at first. But now that so many people have seen the clip, she thinks maybe it could do some good. I told her— well, I kind of told her. What happened. The hat and stuff. She thinks maybe it would help other kids if we could talk about it. Like that kid in Florida."

I froze. Just last week, a news story about a kid being bullied in Florida had gone totally viral. He had snuck in a mini camera and filmed other kids doing stuff like stealing his lunch and kicking his chair. Taylor didn't even like when I *spoke* to Haddie, so I could only imagine how she would react if I painted Taylor as some big bully and Haddie like an innocent victim. Crying, like that Florida kid.

"I don't know," I replied. "I mean, I don't want to make Taylor look like this jerk . . ."

"She's not even in the video," said Haddie. "It wouldn't be about her. I'm not going to say her name or anything. Please, like she *needs* more attention than she gets now."

"How can you even really talk about it then?"

"I don't think they want to put some twelve-year-old's name in the national news like that. In such a negative *way*, you know? I think it's more the idea of a bully than who it actually was."

"You don't think they're going to want to know the name of the—the bullies or whatever?" I asked, skeptical.

"I mean, I just won't say. I'm not trying to get her kicked out of school or anything. And besides, it's not like she was the only one there."

Well. We both knew what that meant. That guilt-weed

in my stomach was turning into a guilt-forest.

"Sorry," Haddie said. "I know you're friends with her . . ."

"She's nice once you get to know her," I said.

Silence.

"Well, anyway. My mom said she's going to give permission. She's talking to one of the producers tomorrow. Then, I think if your dad says it's okay, they're going to come out on Monday. But I told Mom I didn't think your dad would go for it."

"He's on the phone with Principal Howe right this second," I said.

"She's probably trying to get him to join an extra-curricular," said Haddie. "They're Step One to an Enriched Life, you know. That's what the poster in her office says."

"He could join Just Say No. Teach sixth graders not to smoke pot," I said, giggling.

"Or climbing club. Remember when he had to get Mrs. Caldwell's cat out of that tree last year?" Haddie laughed.

"Anything but Future Fashionistas. That blue polyester . . . it's a yikes," I said.

We laughed. *Real* laughs.

"Will you be in school tomorrow?" I asked.

"I actually have an interview with *Wake Up Wisconsin* in the morning. They called my mom."

"Well, I'll keep you posted on what Dad says," I said. Then, "Hey, Haddie?"

"Yeah?"

"I'm . . ." I bit my lip.

Sorry.

Thankful.

Embarrassed.

"Glad you're okay," I said. "Really."

"Thanks, Kate," she said quietly. "I wouldn't be if it wasn't for you."

When my dad came out of his room, he just looked tired.

"You okay?" I asked.

He flopped next to me on the couch. "How are the Badgers?"

"Up by twelve. Michigan's terrible this year."

"Good," he said. But I could tell he wasn't really paying attention to the game.

"Dad . . ."

"Kate," he interrupted me. "In all this craziness . . . I mean, we never really settled on what *you* think of the situation."

"About *The Morning Buzz*?"

"About all of it. About letting people know your name. About being featured as some kind of hero. It could be a good thing for you. And for other people, more importantly. Showing kids out there who get picked on that there's hope. And . . ." His face changed a little, from pride to wariness. "You didn't tell me the full story, Bird. Principal Howe said Haddie's mom told her she was on the ice because of something with a hat? She said a group was bullying her. Were those your friends? Taylor and them?"

"*No.* It wasn't—I mean, it wasn't *bullying*, Dad. It was a joke that got out of hand."

"That's not bullying?" he asked skeptically.

"It was Brett. He's an idiot. Taylor laughed at it. But it wasn't like they were trying to get her killed."

"But what if . . . I mean, during the interview, don't you think they're going to ask Haddie who it was?"

"Dad, Haddie's not going to ruin somebody's life like that."

"But they almost ruined *her* life, didn't they?"

Well, she's a better person than they are is what I really wanted to say. Instead I just shrugged.

"Anyway. My point is, Haddie's mom gave her permission. And since your name is already out there, the damage is kind of done. I was really upset with your mom. I don't think she really thought through the impact of her actions, which, as you know, is something she struggles with in general."

I gestured around the apartment. "Yeah, no duh."

My dad's face fell for a minute, and I suddenly felt bad. He'd rearranged his whole life for me to move in. The least I could do was be a little grateful.

"So does that mean you're saying yes?" I asked.

"I guess I'm saying yes if *you're* saying yes," he said.

My phone buzzed. I glanced down and saw an email notification. It was from my mom's True U account, which I'd tried to unsubscribe from a thousand times.

I opened it, suddenly staring at a photo of her standing next to a *Welcome to Utah* sign.

I'm so excited for this new chapter in my journey as a beauty consultant. My entire life, I've lived for other people. I've given up everything to support others, to raise them up, and to serve, serve, serve. But I'm ready to make the right choices for ME and finally step into my spotlight!

She'd given up everything?

To support *me*?

The mornings I'd crawled into her bed and we'd

spent hours watching *Say Yes to the Dress*, the movie nights where we'd melted entire sticks of butter to pour over our popcorn, the days she'd busted me out of school just to take me to lunch, our trip to the Northwoods . . . that was all just her *giving up everything*? Was I just some pause on her way to True happiness?

Well, guess what? I could step into my spotlight too.

"I'm saying yes."

THE NEXT DAY AT SCHOOL FELT PRETTY NORMAL. HADDIE wasn't there, but over lunch, Taylor pulled up the clip of her on *Wake Up Wisconsin* to show us.

"I'm just really thankful Kate was there," Haddie was saying. "She's the kind of friend who always has your back, and I don't know what would have happened if she hadn't been around."

It was the same anchor who'd been talking when they aired the pond video yesterday—Kyle Something-or-Other.

"You've chosen not to publicly name the kids who were tormenting you. Do you think that the bullies have learned anything from this unfortunate incident?" he asked. I saw Taylor kind of tense up, her hand gripping the phone a little tighter.

"Well, I have to go to school with them tomorrow," said Haddie, looking straight at the camera. "So I sure as heck hope so."

The clip ended and Taylor clicked away with an eye roll. "Somebody thinks she's a celebrity."

"I can't believe she called us bullies. Are we in kindergarten?" asked Violet, biting at a hangnail.

Now that the story was being spun into a bully thing, I was pretty sure Taylor wished she had never shared the video. She had insisted that *Wake Up Wisconsin* wanted to do an interview with her, too, but she said her dad thought it was best to let them focus on Haddie. I couldn't help but wonder if it was really because everyone would be asking what the heck Taylor was doing there. Was she being picked on, too, or was she one of the bullies? Or just an innocent bystander? Better not to let people guess.

"Right?" said Taylor. "My mom sent me this article about how they now have all these laws about bullying in France. Like, calm down."

"You sent your mom the video?" I asked, surprised. Taylor didn't talk about her mom. Ever. Just like I didn't talk about True U.

She turned to me, eyes narrowed. "Yeah. So?"

My heart broke for Taylor Tobitt, for just that instant. I could see it: her sending a video across the ocean. Her own voice, talking about kids being nice, about bravery and courage and heroic rescue. Getting back . . . an article. I wondered for an instant if that's why she took the video in the first place, put it on Facebook, sent it to Channel 6: a hope that her mom, all the way in France, would see it and think of her.

"All of us are bullies but Kate, of course. Her dearest friend," said Brett, batting his eyelashes.

Taylor laughed. It wasn't the fake laugh Haddie had given on the phone, or the real one we'd had talking about my dad. It was a mean laugh, a cut-through-glass laugh, a laugh that made your heart stop. "Yeah. BFFs, with matching bracelets, right?"

My chest tightened. I never should have told Taylor about that stupid bracelet.

"We're not even friends," I said. "I just didn't want her to *die*."

"Whatever you say, BFF," sang Taylor, her voice drenched in syrupy-sweet fakeness. Violet and Amira laughed.

"Why didn't she call you out?" Brett asked Taylor.

"Because how was she supposed to do that without calling out her bestie too?" said Taylor, rolling her eyes.

My heart stopped. I mean, I literally tried to remember what we had learned about heart attacks in health class. Was that the real reason Haddie didn't want to share who all was there? Because she didn't want me to get in trouble? After everything I'd done to her?

"Maybe you should eat at *her* lunch table," said Violet, nodding toward the empty table Haddie usually sat at. "It's ready and waiting for you."

Eat lunch alone? Not with my friends? Be the new one everyone made fun of?

"We're *not* friends. She's so weird. I don't know why she said that," I said.

"Then tell her," said Taylor.

"What?" I asked.

"Tell her. Text her right now and say you don't know why she said you were friends on TV," said Taylor. She pointed to my phone.

"Um." Everyone was looking at me.

"Geez, Taylor, chill," said Amira. "Who cares what Haddie Marks said on TV?"

"You mean the superstar," said Nico, shooting his empty lunch bag toward the garbage and missing.

"Nice air shot," said Brett before burping in Nico's face.

"You guys are gross," I said, happy to change the subject.

"Text her, Kate," said Taylor, staring me down. She wasn't letting this go. I should have known. Taylor could get anything she wanted. She could cause friendships to burst into flames. Taylor snapped her fingers and mountains moved.

My heart started beating really quickly.

"I . . ."

"No phones, guys. Put them away, please." It was Mr. Collins. I could have thrown my arms around him. He might as well have been a Jonas brother. I quickly grabbed my phone and stuck it in my backpack. Everyone else did the same.

"By the way, Kate," Mr. Collins said, "my nephew sent me the video clip of you saving Haddie. He said it was trending on Twitter. That was really incredible. If you want to write something about it for the *Knightly News*, we'd love to publish it."

I shrugged. "Not much to say, really."

"Enough to give a *Morning Buzz* interview, I hear," he said with a smile. "Just think about it."

"I will."

As he walked away, the bell rang. Taylor grabbed her bag and went to class without saying goodbye.

On Monday morning, a hair and makeup crew got to my house at eight.

A short woman introduced herself to me as Meghan

and got to work on my face. My dad stood there nervously watching. He'd taken the day off work and everything.

"I'll be in the room the entire interview," he said, just like he'd told me a thousand times the night before. The producer, JC, was wearing a backward baseball cap and standing in the crowded apartment living room messing with the curtains and the lights. The plan was for an at-home interview in the morning, followed by a few shots of me at school. They'd be filming Haddie after school got out.

"I *know*, Dad," I said.

"And if Maria asks a question you don't want to answer, just simply say, 'I'm not answering that.' It's not live. They can edit it."

"Dad. Stop."

"Please quit talking," Meghan murmured, rubbing some highlighter onto my cheeks.

When she was done, I glanced in the mirror she had set up.

I looked like me, just prettier and bolder. Not like a clown or a movie star. Mostly, my face was really, really tan.

"I know it looks kind of funny. But you'll be under really bright lights for the interview," said Meghan with a smile. "The makeup will make you not look like a ghost."

"My friend Violet would love it," I said. "She always wears, like, a ton of makeup."

Meghan laughed. "Is that . . . is that her? The girl you saved from the ice?"

"No. Different friend."

She nodded. "I remember makeup in seventh grade seeming so fun. Me and my friends would ride our bikes to CVS and spend all our babysitting money on different-flavored lip balms. Dr Pepper and Orange Crush . . . all this silly stuff. Do girls still wear that kind of thing?"

I wasn't a big makeup person. It's not like my parents wouldn't let me. Mom was always trying to convince me to try some True-ly Sparkly Gloss or Be-U-tiful Enchanted Eye Pencil. In the fall, for picture day, she'd offered to give me a makeover. I just hated the way the makeup felt, being patted onto my face with brushes and sponges. It was like I was being painted. I felt . . . wet, yet somehow chalky at the same time. Mom walked me through every step, explaining how she was blending blush and using 4D mascara.

"All right," she had said, all excited. "Take a look!"

When I looked in the mirror, I didn't even recognize

myself. I felt like a little kid at a carnival with their face painted. My cheeks were too red, my forehead too shiny, my eyelids too black, my lips too pink. I wanted to wash it all off immediately.

"You look so beautiful," Mom had said, practically tearing up. All I could think was, if she thought I looked beautiful like *that*, what did she think I looked like the rest of the time? Did she think this was what I needed to look nice?

When I got to school, I went straight to the bathroom and scrubbed my face with paper towels. Taylor had lent me some lip gloss that was pretty simple.

Mom never asked to see my school picture, anyway.

"I don't really wear makeup," I told Meghan, being snapped back to the present. "But I like what you did. I think it looks nice."

She smiled, clipping her makeup case shut. "Good. I'm glad you like it."

"My mom sells makeup. True U," I said.

I saw her freeze for just a second. It was small, but I saw it.

"I'm sure she knows her stuff," Meghan said.

The lights were finally all set up, and JC finished prepping me and my dad on what to expect.

"Maria's on her way here," he said. "She's really

excited to meet you. You guys will do a basic breakdown of who you are, what happened on the ice, if you have any messages for kids being bullied . . . that kind of thing. Piece of cake."

"And I'll be in the room," Dad said. For the millionth time.

"Absolutely," JC said. For the millionth time.

When Maria Ramirez came in, it felt how seeing someone you've watched on TV eight thousand times should feel, I guess. This person, who I'd spotted on the cover of magazines and in tons of YouTube videos, was right there in my living room.

I wasn't sure if she'd be some mega diva, demanding room-temperature bottled water and having a guy follow her around with a fan or grapes or something. But she just smiled and shook my hand.

"Have you ever been interviewed before?" she asked.

"Nope," I said.

"Well, don't you worry. I've done this tons of times. I'll walk you through it. Besides, a girl like you, risking her life to save someone else? An interview's probably a walk in the park," she assured me.

We sat down in some chairs that the crew had brought. Apparently, my dad's secondhand pleather sofa wasn't going to cut it for *The Morning Buzz*. The lights

105

were so bright, I felt like I could barely see Maria's face. And there were more people in Dad's apartment than there ever had been—JC, two guys holding mikes, a woman with a huge camera, and Maria's assistant, who looked just a little younger than my dad.

"Kate, tell me a little bit about yourself," said Maria, with a kind smile. "Introduce yourself to the audience."

I swallowed nervously. "I'm Kate McAllister. I'm in seventh grade at East Middle School, I'm on the basketball team, and I spend most of my time hanging out with my friends."

"Can you tell us what went through your head this week when you saw your best friend, Haddie, fall through the ice on Woodglen Pond?" asked Maria, her face getting more serious.

"Um." I fidgeted a bit. I glanced away at JC, who gave me an encouraging thumbs-up.

"I guess . . . I was scared. I was *really* scared. It was warming up outside, but I knew that falling through ice was still really dangerous. I'd read an article once in a magazine that talked about how quickly you could get hypothermia."

She asked me a couple more questions: which magazine, how I lay on the ice, how cold it felt on my skin.

"But what made you decide to risk your own life

to go and save her? It was such a courageous choice for anyone, let alone a twelve-year-old. What was the moment when you thought, 'I'm going out there'?"

It wasn't a moment.

It was a thousand moments, big, small, in between. It was Haddie in first grade, teaching me the ABCs in sign language on the school bus. It was the time her mom took us to a ballet in second grade and we'd worn matching pink dresses, the kind that left sparkles behind everywhere we sat. It was the time in fifth grade when Laila Johansson told me my nose looked like a ski slope and Haddie "accidently" knocked her milk carton onto Laila's lap. It was the night our electricity got shut off last January, and Mom was in some fight with Dad and didn't want to tell him, so I'd slept at Haddie's in her trundle bed, telling her how much I hated True U and wished my life was ordinary and that I could turn back the clock so my mom could have a normal job and we could live in a subdivision, not a teensy apartment underneath some undergrads.

But more than any of those moments, it was the knowledge, tucked deep into my heart, that there was a right thing to do and a wrong thing to do, and when you have that *knowing*, the choice is yours. And I just wanted to make the right one.

"I don't even remember," I said. "It was more like instinct kicked in."

"Of course," said Maria, nodding. "But were you at all afraid what the other kids were going to say? Apparently there were some kids that had been giving Haddie a hard time. Bullying her, even."

I wanted to open my mouth and defend Taylor, but that *knowing*? It was still there. Burning in my throat. Taylor and Brett and Violet, tossing that hat, Amira doing nothing. They had been horrible. I knew it, and Haddie knew it, and they even knew it, too, probably. And suddenly I wanted the world to know it.

And yet. Taylor, telling me at our first sleepover that I was her best friend in the world.

"Sometimes, it isn't about whose side you're on," I said. "It's not even about sides. It's about making sure everyone's okay. Like, you just kind of . . . know what to do, and you do it. I'm not the kind of person who runs into burning buildings and saves people, or even the kind of person who does big speeches or fancy interviews. I'm just a kid who saw someone in danger and wanted to make sure they were okay."

Maria nodded. "Thank goodness there are girls out there like you, Kate. Because I have to say, I think plenty of people *know* what to do, but they lack the

courage to do it. It's just great, I think. Kate the Great."
She smiled, and I smiled back, and for a second, I felt
like I really was that Good Person everyone thought
I was. It was nice, to lean into your own goodness, to
wear it like a label.

"Cut," said JC. He turned to me. "Kate, that was
absolutely perfect. You're a natural."

"I was nervous," I told Maria as she took a long
swig of water.

"You were great," she said. "I meant what I said."

We snapped a quick selfie together that she immediately had her assistant post to Instagram—after my
dad asked her not to tag me—and then Maria took off,
leaving a cloud of perfume in her wake.

"So, for the rest of the day, we just want to snag
some B-roll. You at school, you with Haddie, you guys
at lunch . . . whatever."

Lunch? *You guys at lunch* . . . as if lunch was just
a boring chunk of time during the day—a meal, not a
battlefield where seventh-grade reputations are decided.
Where was I supposed to sit at lunch? My old table
or my new one? Maybe I could fake a stomachache or
something.

"We told Principal Howe we wouldn't get in the
way too much," he continued. "We'll talk to her, and

Haddie as well, then do a quick edit tonight, and this is going to air during our seven thirty segment tomorrow morning," JC explained to Dad and me while the cameraman packed up.

"Sounds great," Dad said. "Thank you so much. I hope this does a lot of good for other kids."

"I'm sure it will," JC said, glancing at his watch. "You should be proud of your daughter."

"I am. And not just because of this five seconds of fame."

As Dad drove me to school, JC following behind, I pulled out my phone and sent Mom the selfie of Maria and me.

So proud of u!! she texted back almost immediately.

I miss you, I wrote honestly.

Me too, she wrote. *More than u know.*

IT WAS WEIRD, SEEING HADDIE ON HER FIRST DAY BACK.

"Hey," she said with a slow smile as she slid into her desk in homeroom.

"Hey," I told her.

"How was your interview?" she asked.

"Um. Good. How was yours?"

"It's not till after school."

"Right."

It felt like we were trying to remember a dance we'd learned a long time ago. Bumping elbows and falling over, remembering our inside jokes and how to talk to someone who had been your best friend for six years.

The morning went by pretty typically, just with a camera kind of hanging out in the back of each classroom. It sat and blinked at me while I worked on pre-algebra and translated Spanish verbs. Kids kept trying to jump in the background, waving and giving peace signs to the cameras. I made sure not to ask any questions or anything.

When I saw Taylor in science, things seemed back to normal-ish. I thought maybe she'd be mad about yesterday, with the phone and everything, but she didn't say a word about it. In fact, she showed me how she'd redecorated her binder, putting a photo of the two of us front and center. I did notice she sat on the side of our lab station that was closer to the camera and she kept flipping her hair.

By the time science ended and lunch rolled around, I was ready for the whole thing to be over. But just as I was about to claim I didn't feel well, Taylor grabbed my arm, squeezing it tight.

"Gonna swing by my locker. See you at lunch," she said cheerfully.

"Actually . . . ," I started, but JC cut me off.

"Perfect," he said. "We'll make sure to get some shots of you and Haddie."

Taylor looked at me, surprised. But then, I could see it—*click*—like a key turning in her brain. She winked at me.

She understood.

"See you," I told her, a million *thank-you*s underneath my words.

I walked into the cafeteria with the camera crew, greeted by the smell of melting nacho cheese. Then, I went to Haddie's table and sat down as if I did that every day. She had on a way-too-big tie-dyed T-shirt. It looked like something you'd make at summer camp or a family reunion. I had a sinking feeling in the pit of my stomach: that guilt ache, settling in and making itself comfortable. My fake stomachache was now entirely real. JC and the camera handler plopped down a few feet away from us. Any shiny feelings I'd had from my Maria Ramirez interview were gone. It was easy to play the hero with someone who didn't know who you really were. It was a lot harder to do it with someone whose house you've slept over at more times than you can count.

"Hey," I said. Was she going to ask me what the heck I was doing there?

She looked surprised, but only for a second. Then, she looked happy. *So* happy, like Houa did after making a three-pointer.

That made me feel even worse.

"Hey," she said happily, stabbing her fork into that day's mystery meat. "What's up?"

"Not . . . a lot." I opened up my paper bag and took out the lunch I'd quickly made myself that morning.

Dad had insisted on making my lunch when I first moved in, but honestly, bologna? It was pretty obvious he'd never lived with a twelve-year-old girl for more than a weekend.

"You start your history project yet?" she asked.

"No. I have Marquis de Lafayette. You?"

"Mercy Otis Warren." We each had to do an oral report on an influential person from the Revolutionary War. It was due at the end of the month.

"Cool," I said.

"Yeah. I have no idea who she is, but I guess I'll find out."

"I feel like not a lot of people got women. I heard Brett say he got Abigail Adams, and he said he was going to give his report in a dress."

"He would," said Haddie with an eye roll. "And, like, lipstick." I didn't say anything, and then I realized—I was waiting for her to make a joke. Whenever we talked about makeup at Taylor's lunch table, it was always followed by someone saying something snarky about Mom being the True U lady. But Haddie didn't take any thrill from embarrassing me.

So why did Taylor?

"How long have you been staying with your dad?" she asked.

My face got hot and I saw JC raise his eyebrows at my obvious awkwardness. He was probably wondering why my alleged best friend didn't know where I lived.

"Is a chat about our history projects really *Morning Buzz* material?" I asked him. I felt like everyone in the cafeteria was talking a little extra loudly. People were walking by and staring at the camera too. Mollie Graf had thrown, like, eighteen things away because we were kind of near a garbage can.

"B-roll," he said. "You know. Shots we can play to show your guys' friendship. But I'm going to grab a soda quick." He hopped up and went to the soda machine, and the dude holding the biggest camera fiddled with it for a second. I turned to Haddie and grabbed her wrist.

"Stop talking about my parents," I hissed out.

"Geez. Okay. I was just wondering," she said, her eyes looking hurt.

"Well, stop. It's nobody's business."

"*Okay.*"

Suddenly, Taylor appeared out of nowhere, sliding next to me.

"Hey," she chirped. "Mind if I join?"

"Kind of," said Haddie flatly.

"*No,*" I said. "Of course not."

Taylor took a long sip of her iced tea and tucked her

hair behind her ears. "So, Haddie, how are you feeling?"

Haddie opened her mouth to reply, but JC was back, taking his seat. She glanced at him, then at me, then back at Taylor.

That stupid camera. If only it was around all the time. Then people would actually be nice to each other. Maybe that's what we need, cameras following us around and making a documentary about the sucky lives of seventh graders. But is that even really being nice? Or is that just putting on a show? Isn't being kind how you act when *The Morning Buzz* isn't around?

Then . . . who was kind?

Was Taylor?

Was Haddie?

Was I?

"I'm fine," Haddie decided on. "Thanks to Kate."

Taylor smiled. Reading Taylor was like reading another language. It took time and *práctica*, as Señora De La Rosa would have said. A Taylor smile could mean a million different things, but I knew this one. I'd seen it before, aimed at obnoxious boys or Not-Mom Stephanie, or even at Violet, a time or two.

It said, *Don't mess with me.*

"I'm Taylor Tobitt," she said smoothly, turning to JC, who nodded. "I'm the one who took the video." She had extra eyeliner on today, I noticed. My mom would be impressed.

"Oh wow! The famous Taylor," said JC. "So, you must have seen the bullies, too, then."

The bullies. As if they were strangers who hid under our beds instead of right inside our East Middle School Knights hoodies. People who snuck up behind us instead of people we asked to pass the Bunsen burner. *Bullies* could like your photo on Instagram five seconds before they spread a rumor about you or made fun of your hair.

"If you ask me, it was more like a joke that got out of hand than it was *bullying*," said Taylor. "Kids around here would never bully anybody. We're not like those Florida kids, you know? Midwest-nice and all that?"

"Right . . . ," said JC. I hadn't known him very long—only a few hours. But I suddenly realized that JC was fluent in Taylor too.

Because *his* smile said, *I don't buy that for a second.*

"I actually have to go," I said suddenly. "Bathroom. Then I need to go study for a little bit in the library. I'll . . . I'll talk to you guys later."

I jumped up and booked it before JC could follow, leaving Haddie and Taylor in my wake. They made an unlikely pair. When I got to the lunchroom doors,

117

I looked back, and they were still there, talking. I had no idea about what.

"Kate! It's starting."

It was early the next morning. I shoved one more bite of cereal into my mouth before going to sit on the couch next to Dad.

"And now," said the main anchor, "a story that's been creating *buzz* across the nation. Maria Ramirez, take it away."

"In an age group plagued by bullying, one student in Madison, Wisconsin, is working to change the tide." Maria's voice played as clips of Haddie and me talking at lunch and walking down the hall flashed across the screen. "Kate McAllister, a seventh grader, is being heralded as a hero for saving her best friend from bullies and pulling her out of an icy pond."

The segment started, and there were our faces, unblurred. Haddie looked terrified.

I looked . . . determined. I looked *strong*. I looked nothing like myself.

Next were a few clips of my interview, along with some statistics about bullying. They showed my school picture, which made me freeze—Mom was going to see me without any of her True U makeup on.

Haddie's mom, Juliet, was suddenly onscreen, her eyes serious and her hair pulled back tightly.

"The thing that upsets me the most is that these kids aren't even going to be punished. Some people might think it's just a joke that went too far. But we need to remember that someone could have been seriously hurt. And one of these days, they're going to be," Juliet said. "Haddie says she didn't see who specifically threw her hat out on the ice. But we know which kids were *there*. And I wish more of them were being questioned."

Uh-oh.

Finally, they played a clip of Haddie's interview.

"Haddie, what would you say to other kids who are experiencing bullying?"

Haddie looked toward the camera. "I would tell them that bullies always get what they deserve, in the end." It was as if she was looking right at me. "And that you should focus on who your *true* friends are. Because if you have just one of those—even if it's only yourself— you'll be okay."

I thought they'd end it there, but the tape cut back to my interview. I wondered if Mom was watching.

"I'm just a kid who saw someone in danger and wanted to make sure they were okay," I said to the camera.

119

You took Haddie's words, and then you took mine: they told a story. A story of two best friends standing up against the Powers That Be, the bullies you see in comics and the types of movies they show you in assemblies.

But what if that story wasn't true? What if there was an imposter who looked like a hero, the way you can add a filter to a selfie?

The camera was back on the main anchor.

"Kate the Great," he said with a smile. "We're all thankful for the bit of sunshine you've given us this morning. Now, on to Alicia Strickland with an update on the situation in Iran."

Dad picked up the remote and turned the TV off. "Wow. Kate the Great."

I rolled my eyes. "Yikes."

"Hey . . . Bird?"

"Yeah, Dad?"

"You know I'm proud of you, right? For what you did for Haddie? And for going on TV and talking about it?"

"Yeah," I said. "Of course I do."

"Okay. Good. But, um . . . I also—I wanted to know . . . why *were* you there? I've been going over it in my head, and there's something that's not . . . adding up. Were you there with Haddie? Because I know you haven't really hung out with her in a while."

I froze.

"Which is fine!" he said quickly. "Friendships change. I get it. But . . . Taylor just seems kind of—I don't know, bossy?"

"What makes you say that?" I said, defensive. "You don't even know her."

"I don't know, that time with the Halloween costumes . . ."

So, here's part of the problem of becoming friends with a girl you kind of hated before: you probably told your parents things about her that they'll never forget. In sixth grade, Haddie and I were sushi rolls for Halloween, which was actually pretty cute. But Haddie still wanted to go trick-or-treating, and even though I didn't want to, because we were obviously too old, I went anyway, because what else was I supposed to do? Sit at home alone? And of course we avoided Taylor's house, but of course she was at Amira's, and we didn't know where Amira lived. Even though Amira's mom was really nice and gave us king-size candy bars, I saw Taylor, Amira, and Violet just behind her, giggling into their hands, and asking us if we went to East Elementary just to be jerks, even though Violet sat next to me in English every single day.

And had I told Dad on the phone the next day, ranting about how mean they were, and how immature Haddie was, and how stupid Halloween is in general because it was obviously just invented by a candy company?!

You bet.

"That was a million years ago," I snapped.

"I mean, I guess I'm just trying to ask—do you know who threw her hat out on the ice? Was it your group of friends?"

Was it?

Was it Violet?

Was it me?

"And if it was, I just want you to tell me, okay? I'm not going to tell anyone or get anyone in trouble. I just want to know," Dad said quietly. "You were there, Bird, and there weren't *that* many kids . . . I mean, you had to have seen something."

My dad had people lie to him every single day. He was a professional lie sniffer-outer. I had to be honest.

"I don't know," I said. And it *was* honest.

"You don't know?" he asked gently.

"No. I don't know. We were laughing, and I thought Haddie was laughing too, and her hat was on her head, and then it wasn't, and . . . I don't know, Dad. It all happened so fast."

"Okay," he said calmly. "Okay. If you're sure you don't know."

"I don't know," I said again. "I don't *know*."

He nodded. "Well, then let's go to school, huh? I need to get to work." He plopped a kiss on my head. "I'm so proud of you, Bird. I am."

I didn't know, I reminded myself as I zipped up my backpack, tightened my ponytail, and grabbed my coat.

I didn't know.

10

AND SUDDENLY, EVERYONE WAS LOOKING AT ME.

I get stared at . . . more than the average seventh grader. I'm tall, for one. I stand out. Plus, I'm usually with Taylor and Violet and Amira. They get looked at because Taylor is pretty and loud, a combination that attracts a lot of eyes. So I'm looked at too. But not like this. Not like walking down the hallway with everyone glancing from the corners of their eyes, not like teachers poking their heads out their classroom doors. Teachers I don't even know. Mrs. Shiloh, Amira's English teacher who she hated, took a photo of me as I walked by. I swear.

"Beyoncé!" squealed Taylor as I walked into the lunchroom. I almost looked around for Mrs. Urbanski. Then I realized: she meant *me*. She threw her arms around me and I coughed as the smell of her lavender-lilac body spray squeezed into my lungs.

"Hey," I laughed.

"Your majesty," said Nico, bowing low. Brett held up his phone to take fake paparazzi pictures.

"What the heck?" I asked.

"You're trending," sang Amira, shoving her phone in my face. I grabbed the phone and looked at Twitter.

#KateTheGreat

I scrolled and scrolled. *The Morning Buzz* clips were retweeted over and over, from news station profiles and normal people's accounts and—oh my gosh—that country singer my mom loved. I watched myself pulling Haddie out of the pond, over and over, and then there was my face, smiling at Maria Ramirez.

"Phones away, guys," said Señora De La Rosa, walking by, but smiling.

"Kate!" Haddie ran over, her eyes shining. "We're *everywhere*! Cory Freaking Seymour just featured the clip of you on *The Morning Buzz* in his Instagram story!"

Taylor practically spat out the iced tea she had just sipped.

"Cory Seymour?" I asked. "Are you sure? This is incredible." I felt excited, sure, but more embarrassed. Kate the Great? It sounded like a superhero name. Not *me*, who just rebounded basketballs, read a lot, helped her mom organize mascaras.

Haddie grinned. I noticed that our group was kind of *looking* at her, not with a look of *Eww, get away from our lunch table*, but a look of—something else. Curiosity, maybe. Like they were wondering what she was going to say next. Like maybe they hadn't really seen her before.

So what was I supposed to do now? I was Kate the Great, not just Kate McAllister. Maybe Kate McAllister made fun of kids and went along with whatever Taylor said. Kate McAllister might have ignored Haddie or rolled her eyes about her excitement at a vlogger.

But Kate the Great was nice. And, whatever, we *liked* that vlogger.

So I grinned back. But before I could even say anything, Amira jumped in.

"I think it's really cool," she said, twisting the top off a bottle of juice. "I'm kind of sick of hearing about how mean middle schoolers are."

"Yeah," said Nico. "Your interview was kinda cool too, Haddie. I watched it this morning."

Haddie blushed, and it almost made me feel worse. That small statement—that teensy acceptance—meant so much to her. It was like all the times Nico had called her Haddie Marko-weird were erased.

"You guys looked great," said Taylor. "Was that True U makeup?"

It was one of those mean-not-mean comments, said so casually that the other person isn't really allowed to get mad. You'd almost rather someone just call you a jerk to your face or say something you could get worked up about instead of something so underhanded. Because, again—what could we do? Just smile. Laugh, even. Part of me was . . . How did I feel? *Mad.* So mad, *furiously* mad at Taylor in that moment. But that fierce fire of anger at her was nothing compared to the anger I felt at myself, when I did what I did next:

Smiled.

Because if I didn't, it would be worse. Worse than a jab at my weird mom. Worse than a hat thrown onto a pond? I don't know, maybe. But I was so tired, and the easy thing—to smile back—was right there.

And Taylor grinned back—a grin of victory. Some sort of silent exchange had taken place—her taking power, and me giving it, over and over and over again.

My last class of the day was computer literacy, which I hated. As soon as Ms. Anyanwu was distracted, I pulled out my phone.

Casey Whalen, True U Beauty Consultant, hadn't

posted on Instagram the past two days. She didn't have anything new in her feed, but when I clicked on Stories, there it was—a short clip of the pond video, a clip of me talking to Maria, and then me—just me. A picture of me at our old apartment, not really looking that great, sprawled across the couch. Smiling.

So proud of my baby girl!!! the caption said. *I knew she was great and now the WORLD does too. She truly EXEMPLIFIES what it means to STEP INTO YOUR SPOTLIGHT!!*

Then her story changed. A graphic for a True U sale. Buy-one-get-one-free eyeshadow palettes.

Mom hadn't texted me. Or called me. Or anything.

And there it was again—anger.

Look, I'm not an angry person. I'm usually pretty smiley. I won Most Cheerful in fifth grade, and I still have the stupid cardboard certificate in a box in my closet. *Kate's so easygoing, always so polite*—that's what people told my parents. I don't get *mad* at people very often. Even when Mom missed my sixth-grade basketball tournament because she had a True U house party, or when she and Dad got in big fights over the phone, or when Haddie's cousin Willow saw me at the grocery store a month ago and said something snarky about how I'd "changed."

But that feeling, that rage, was there. It was bubbling up and boiling over. I was mad—mad at my mom for leaving, and mad at Taylor for being so mean sometimes and then nice five seconds later, and mad at Haddie for going out onto the ice. I was mad at Maria Ramirez. I was so mad that I couldn't just sit at that computer anymore or I would burst into a million pieces. I didn't feel like Kate the Great.

"I have to go to the bathroom," I told Ms. Anyanwu. Some kids needed a bathroom pass, but I was one of those Good Kids. Kate McAllister, and especially Kate the Great, wouldn't cut class to roam the halls. So I could pee whenever I wanted. Ms. Anyanwu just waved her hand; she was busy teaching Tony Doyle how to find some file he'd downloaded. I took off, planning on just walking a couple of laps.

East Middle School was like any other school. Rows of lockers. A trophy case. It smelled like hot dogs, no matter what time of day it was. There was the teachers' lounge, a science lab, and the creaky auditorium. Bulletin boards filled with "exemplary schoolwork." And then there was Dad.

Wait, what? *Dad*, standing in the hallway, awkwardly chatting with Mr. Krall-Ryan, who taught eighth-grade math. Dad had had him for eighth-grade math at this very same school, in that very same classroom.

"Dad?" I asked.

They both turned to me, surprised.

"Kate," said Dad. "What are you doing in the hall?"

"What are *you* doing in the hall?"

"I should get back in," said Mr. Krall-Ryan, glancing back into his classroom. "They'll be finishing up that pop quiz." *Likes pop quizzes*, I filed away, in case I got him for math next year. "Good to see you, Sam."

He went back into his classroom and Dad took me by the arm. "Why aren't you in class?"

"Bathroom. Are you working?" He had his police uniform on.

"Technically, yeah, but Principal Howe also called. I just got done talking with her. She's wondering if they should launch an investigation into . . . the incident."

"An investigation? What do you mean?" *Oh no. Bad. Bad-bad-bad.*

"Bird, this is a big deal. And Haddie said it happened because kids were picking on her. I think the principal has every right to figure out who it was. But it wasn't on school property, and besides, she talked to Haddie and her mom, and Haddie is adamant about not naming names or blaming anyone."

"I already told Principal Howe who was there," I said.

"Yeah, I know. But Haddie won't confirm they did anything. So what's Principal Howe supposed to do?" Dad ran a hand through his hair. "I didn't realize . . . you're *everywhere*. The entire department was talking about it. I should have known it was going to go viral. Are you okay? Are you holding up?"

"It wasn't a clip of me robbing a bank, Dad. People think I'm some kind of hero."

He shook his head. "Those expectations, though. They can be . . . a lot. I wanted to see if you were okay. And also . . . someone called."

"Mom?"

"What?" he asked, confused. "No. Why? Did your mom call *you*?"

"No," I said. "I just—when you said 'someone' . . ."

"Right. Sorry," he said, uncomfortable. "Um . . . no. Haven't heard from Mom in a few days. I'll text her tonight. But . . . that Cory guy you watch on the computer. Cory Seymour?"

I froze. "No."

"Yes. Well, it wasn't *him*; it was his assistant. She said Cory saw the clip and went wild. He thought it was 'legit inspiring' . . . whatever that means. They called *The Morning Buzz* to see if we could get connected. He wants you to come to California."

"Oh my God. Dad! I love him."

"I know. And normally, I'd say no way, José. But . . ." He scratched his neck. "You know Greg?"

"Mustache Greg?" He was Dad's partner, sometimes. Had weird facial hair.

"Yeah. He has a daughter at West Middle. Said she's had such a hard time this year with kids not being nice. And she said that news story gave her . . . hope. That there were people like you who'd—you know. Do the right thing. You should have seen him telling me this, Kate. Thought he was gonna cry right there in the bullpen."

I pictured Mustache Greg's daughter watching the video on her phone. Seeing that brief clip, that one moment in my life—and it meaning so *much* to her.

What if she went to East? Would she eat lunch with me and Taylor? Or would she be another thing for us to laugh at?

"I think this can help kids, Kate," Dad said. "I do. If you want to do this, it's fine by me. But it's a big thing to be prepared for."

"I thought me going viral was your worst nightmare."

"I think you not being around to pull Haddie out of that pond would have been *her* dad's worst nightmare," he said, and he looked serious. Well, okay then. Dad was going to let me do something major on the internet. I should have glanced out the window to see if any pigs were flying.

"I want to do it," I said instantly.

Dad smiled. "Good. They said you can bring a friend too. Flight and hotel and all that paid for. It's something."

"When will we go?"

"Well, they said they'd work with our schedule, but they'd like to do it sooner rather than later, while the story's still everywhere. They were hoping for, like, tomorrow. I've gotta take off work, but I have plenty of days saved up."

I nodded. "Okay. Thanks for telling me. I'm excited. I can't believe . . . I mean, Cory Seymour."

I didn't mean to say what I said next, but it popped right out.

"If Mom were here, we could go out to lunch to celebrate. I wish you had a job like that." It was true, but it also wasn't true. Because I liked that Dad had a job where I could go to the dentist every six months and his lights never got shut off and he didn't try to convince the other dads at school to become cops. And his face fell, for half a second, before he smiled.

"I wish we could do that too. But someone's gotta go catch the bad guys. Besides, we're about to spend two days in California together."

He hugged me, and I wasn't even embarrassed, even though anyone could have walked by. I let him hug me in a deep hug, and I was so thankful for him in that second. Him and that blue polyester.

"I love you, Kate," he said.

"Go catch those bad guys," I replied.

"KATE?" DAD POKED HIS HEAD INTO THE OFFICE, AKA MY room. It was that afternoon, and I was shoving clothes in a duffel bag for our trip the next day. "I called school and told them you weren't going to be there the next two days. I also called Coach, but I convinced her you can still play Saturday."

"Thanks, Dad." Saturday was the third game in the annual Southeastern Wisconsin Girls Basketball Tournament, Middle School Division. It was our last round before state championships. Meaning, if I wasn't there, Coach Watt would have a heart attack. I can't imagine it took much "convincing."

"No prob, Bob," he said, whistling and walking back into the kitchen. For someone who had spent the vast majority of his parenthood being the Weekend Parent, Dad was actually way better at stuff like that than Mom was. He wasn't used to signing permission slips or calling school or driving me home from practice, but he'd picked it all up pretty effortlessly.

We were leaving for California the next morning. Cory Seymour had told me I could bring a friend, but I'd decided not to. I was trying to ignore the fact that Taylor would throw me in Lake Mendota if she found out. Taylor *loved* Cory Seymour, maybe even more than I did.

But there were pieces of Taylor that I didn't know. Even though we'd been friends this year, even though her phone background was a selfie the two of us had taken at her parents' New Year's party—we didn't have that Shared Best Friend History that I had with Haddie. Taylor didn't know that I was afraid of sharks and that when Mom and I won that cruise to Jamaica, I wouldn't even put my feet in the water. She didn't know that when I was in elementary school, I wanted to be a dental hygienist because our neighbor was one and always seemed so happy to go to work. And there were so many things I didn't know about *her*: what she had felt like when her mom moved to Paris, or if *she* was afraid of anything at all. Why she hated Haddie, and why she spread a rumor last fall that David-Michael Thomas was obsessed with Mrs. Urbanski and had a shrine of her in his room. Why she had picked me to be friends with, when she could have picked anyone. And all this not-knowingness: it made me nervous to be around her lately. You could be someone's best friend and also be nervous about who they were as a real, breathing person.

And Haddie . . . well, I could have brought Haddie. That's what Cory Seymour probably expected me to do. Bring my old best friend, the one who didn't make me nervous or cause me to double-triple-quadruple-guess things I said. The one who just *was*, and who let me just *be*, without having to constantly feel like I was performing. With Haddie, I just didn't have to try so hard.

But Taylor would have killed me.

I mean, roadkill-level social death.

So I just didn't tell anyone I could bring a friend to California. I would go with my dad. We'd order room service and meet Cory Seymour, and then soon enough, this would all be over. I could go back to being normal Kate McAllister—not Kate the Great—a boring seventh grader instead of a hashtag in everyone else's timeline.

The apartment intercom buzzed, which made me jump. It took some getting used to, apartment-building life. Mom and I had always lived in rentals, but they were usually shabby places downtown. Dad's apartment felt more like a hotel.

"Who is it?" Dad asked over the intercom.

"Haddie?" She said it like a question.

Dad let her in right away, and a minute or so later, she knocked on our front door.

"Hey," I said, letting her in. "Um . . . what's up?"

"Sorry. I could have texted you or something."

"No, it's cool. I'm just packing."

"I heard. Cory Seymour? That's amazing," said Haddie. I would have asked how she'd heard, but I *had* told Taylor I was going, and once Taylor knew something, it seemed like the rest of the school did too.

"Thanks," I said with a smile.

"I actually—I went to your old apartment first? But there were some college kids in it now. And I know your dad's been driving you to school. So I thought you'd be over here. Do you like . . . live here now?"

I was going to say the same thing I'd been telling Taylor: My mom would be back soon. This was a temporary trip. She was going to reach True Diamond ASAP, and then she'd be back, and we'd be in a different apartment, and everything would go back to normal.

But something stopped me. Because Haddie and I *did* have that shared history. She knew about my shark issue. She'd helped me pack for Jamaica, lent me one of her swimsuits so I didn't have to wear the same one every day, helped Mom and me stuff a bright pink suitcase with business cards and lanyards for her team.

"Yeah," I said. "I am. My mom moved to Utah."

"Oh my gosh. That's . . . that's a lot."

"I know," I said.

"For True U?"

"Yup." I shrugged. "She said she'd come back once she hits True Diamond. So we're just waiting."

"Oh man. What's it like living with your dad?"

I glanced back into the kitchen, where Dad was cracking open a beer and whistling a Beatles song.

"It's good," I said. "Different. But some things about it are good. No body glitter left all over the bathroom counters, for one. And I can walk around in ratty clothes because he doesn't take a thousand Instagram photos."

She grinned. "Yeah. Remember when your mom had us do the intro for her monthly team call?"

"Those *shirts*," I groaned. Matching ones, with glittery *Future Diamond* stickers on them. We'd had to announce to Team Glitter 'n' Glitz that they'd broken the sales record for the month.

"You're *True-ly* amazing women," Haddie sang out.

"More like *True-ly* dumb," I said.

"*True-ly* desperate."

"*True-ly* barf-inducing."

We laughed. Another thing I missed about Haddie—she was funny. Brett spent a lot of time *trying* to be funny, but I hadn't laughed in a way that made my stomach hurt in a while.

"We had fun, though, too, with the True U crap," she reminded me. "Remember when she won that shopping spree at Target and we got all those books?"

"Yeah," I said. "That was great."

"Anyway. I just wanted to swing by and say . . . that the last couple of days have been cool. It's been nice being your friend again."

Were we friends again? Had I fixed everything, just by going out on that ice? Were all my mistakes really just wiped away like a clean slate?

It didn't seem possible. But I suddenly wanted it to be so, so badly. I wanted Haddie to sit with us at lunch, so that someone else could think Violet and Brett were obnoxious. I wanted someone else around who didn't think shampoo brands deserved a full twenty minutes of conversation.

I missed her, even though I felt like I wasn't allowed to. I felt like I didn't *deserve* to. That jar of fireflies, though—maybe they held some magic, after all.

"Hey . . . do you want to come to California?" I asked.

Haddie's eyes were surprised. "What?"

"Cory Seymour. In California. His assistant said I could bring a friend. Sorry it's so . . . last-minute. I mean, you probably can't, right? Because we have to be at the airport at, like, five a.m."

"Come *with* you?" It was like I had handed her a billion dollars. That was how excited she looked. And that made me feel horrible.

"Yeah. If you want."

"Of course!" she squealed. "Oh my God! I'd love to!"

"Dad?" We ducked into the kitchen, where he was unloading the dishwasher. "Can Haddie come to California with us?"

"Come with? I mean, we'd love to have you, Haddie." My dad had always loved Haddie. He said she was the kind of person who wasn't afraid to be who she was. He never said that about me. He probably shouldn't. I *was* afraid to be who I was sometimes. I pretended to like Frappuccinos from Starbucks even though they sort of gave me a headache. One time when Taylor was flipping through my phone for music, she asked me why I had the *Les Misérables* soundtrack, and I told her I added it on accident even though I really love that musical. I didn't wear gloves outside because none of my friends did, even though my hands were freezing. Stuff like that.

"The thing is, though, we told them we weren't bringing anyone else. So she doesn't have a ticket. And it's in less than twelve hours," Dad reminded me. He hadn't been on an airplane since high school. He was antsy—not about the Big Piece of Metal Flying Across the Sky, but about the logistics. When Mom and I flew somewhere, she liked to get us to the airport about thirty minutes before boarding so that we didn't have to wait around. Dad was the kind of person who'd already checked three different routes to the airport on Google Maps and actually put his toiletries in one of those plastic baggies.

"Could we call them?" asked Haddie.

"I mean . . . yeah. I guess I could try. It's just—you know, it's short notice. So we'll see what they say, okay? Haddie, let me call your mom first."

So the calling happened—Dad on the phone with Juliet, and then with Cory's assistant, and then with the airline. And soon we all had boarding passes texted to our phones.

"I have to pack!" squealed Haddie. "I can't believe we're doing this together. This is going to be the best few days of my life. I'm gonna go buy candy for the plane. Swedish Fish?"

"And Sour Patch Kids," I said. "The big kind, like we'd get at the pool."

"Got it. See you bright and early," she said, practically racing out the door.

It had been such a whirlwind. I flopped onto the couch backward, my legs dangling over the edge, and Dad looked at me cautiously.

"I'm gonna ask you something. Don't get mad."

"Okay . . . ," I said, scratching Watson's tummy as he rolled over beneath me.

"Will Taylor be pissed about this?"

Of course she would be. Taylor would be mad, angry, *furious*. Taylor would be filled with white-hot rage. Her eyeballs would pop out of her head.

But that second, I felt a little bit of fire in *my* bones. Taylor would be mad. Fine. Well, I was kind of mad at her too. That True U joke at lunch had been mean, and she knew it. And pretending to be all nice to Haddie at lunch was obnoxious, when she'd been mean to her for forever. I was Taylor's best friend, but that was a hard job, and it was feeling harder and harder, and maybe I needed a day off.

"It'll be fine," I said.

"Something going on there, Bird? Not an expert in middle-school girls. Just saying. I haven't seen Haddie much all year, and you've had a sleepover with Taylor and that crew almost every weekend. Doesn't take a genius. I was in seventh grade once."

"*Dad.* I said it'll be okay."

"Okay! Okay." He put his hands in the air. "I surrender. Let's go to bed early, huh? Got a big flight tomorrow."

After I got ready for bed and went into the office—Dad promising for the millionth time we'd turn it into a real bedroom soon—and after I yanked out the pullout couch and tugged that scratchy blanket up to my chin, I took out my phone, avoiding the stare of Creepy Jesus.

Nothing from Mom. No calls, no texts. Nothing new on Instagram, even. That wasn't like Casey Whalen, True Sapphire. She usually checked in at least three times a day for her two thousand adoring followers.

I glanced out the window. The stars didn't tend to be bright in our area, but tonight, they were putting on a show, twinkling away. I wondered if Mom was looking at them in Salt Lake City.

I'll wear that stupid Future Diamond *T-shirt*, I wanted to tell her. *I'll ask Maria Ramirez about her mascara. I'll do whatever. Just come back. Come back. Come back.*

12

"CHECK OUT THIS *ROOM!*"

I'd stayed in hotels before. Pretty nice ones, even, on trips Mom had won. But I'd never stayed in a *suite.* Here, we had our own living room, and a separate bedroom off to the side with a king-size bed.

"That's for you girls," Dad said, nodding toward it and putting his duffel on the couch. "I'm good out here."

"Are you sure, Dad? We don't mind the couch," I said. Haddie nodded in agreement.

"Nah. You've spent the last couple weeks on a pull-out," he said.

Haddie and I looked at each other and ran into the bedroom, practically shrieking. There was a giant bathroom, too, with—was that a *hot tub?* It reminded me of when we were seven years old and Haddie's mom had taken us to American Girl Place for Haddie's birthday. We thought it was the best day of our lives.

Her mom had a video of us jumping up and down and shrieking when we realized she had bought us dresses that matched our dolls.

"This is *amazing*," squealed Haddie, rolling onto the bed.

"Cory Seymour must be loaded," I said.

"Or he just thinks you're a superstar," said Haddie. "Kate the Great!"

I glanced at my phone. There was a text from Taylor: **OMG, come back. Ms. Irvine is making me dissect a cow eyeball! By MYSELF!** 🤢

I laughed.

"Who is it?" asked Haddie.

"Nobody," I said, tossing my phone into my bag.

I'd lied. Okay? I'd *kind of* lied. I hadn't told Taylor that Haddie was coming. She hadn't exactly asked, but I definitely hadn't offered, and in Taylor's world, failing to tell her anything of even slight importance was a Big Fat Lie.

Of course she was going to find out. Cory Seymour couldn't sneeze without sharing it on Instagram, and the whole *point* of our trip was to film a video with him. But I'd tell her when we got back. I just needed . . . a plan. A plan to make Taylor and Haddie not hate each other.

It seemed sort of impossible. But if I wanted to be

Haddie's friend again *and* I wanted to be Taylor's friend, it made sense. Right? Look, if we can put people on the moon and have ice cream delivered to our front door in under an hour, I think we can find a way to get two archenemies to tolerate each other during lunch period. I needed some of Mom's #GirlBoss, can-do sparkle. I felt it, that blind optimism, that feeling my mom got when she saw the numbers for the month and knew she had to make some sales. I felt as glittery as Mom's eyeshadow. I understood her, in that moment—the willingness to look at the impossible and think, with one swipe of your hand, you can fix it.

"Guys, we have to be there in an hour," Dad said. "Let's get something to eat downstairs and be ready for our car."

The hotel had a pizza place in the lobby, and cheesy carbs sounded like an ideal way to start our adventure. We ordered a giant sausage-and-mushroom while guessing what Cory's house was going to look like. Did he really have a pet baby shark that lived in an indoor swimming pool, or was that just a rumor? By the time the driver picked us up in the huge black car that Cory had sent, we were hyper from soda and checking each other's teeth.

We drove out of the city a bit and into a neighborhood

with gigantic houses. We tried googling where Taylor Swift lived but didn't have any luck.

While Dad chatted with the driver up front, Haddie and I took a ton of selfies together. Taylor was going to be so mad.

"Why?" asked Haddie, a confused look on her face.

Crap. Had I said that out loud?

"She just . . . I don't know. She gets jealous sometimes," I admitted. "She just likes to be the one to always have the coolest experiences, if that makes sense."

Haddie rolled her eyes. "Sounds like a keeper."

"You know," I said, sensing my opening, "I know you think you know Taylor. But she's really not that bad. She's into Cory Seymour videos too."

"She is?" asked Haddie, surprised.

"Heck yeah. She's like, a superfan," I said. "*And* she likes Harry Potter. She's read them all." This, I knew, impressed Haddie.

"Well, she's a total Slytherin," she said.

"I just don't feel like you really give her a chance."

"Kate," Haddie said, clearly starting to get ticked off. She looked at me as if I had just suggested we skip Cory Seymour and go do our homework back at the hotel instead. "Why should I? I can't even tell if you're serious right now. She's the entire reason we're here!"

she said, throwing her arms up.

"What are you talking about?"

"What am I *talking*— Kate, your alleged bestie is a total jerk. News flash."

"*No*, she's not," I said, getting frustrated. This wasn't going according to plan. "I know if you just got to know her—"

"Has she ever tried to get to know *me*? For five seconds?"

"But—"

"I thought maybe, just maybe, you invited me here because you finally saw how terrible your quote-unquote *friends* are. That when they—you know, did what they *did* the other day, you'd dump them. But, wow. I guess I was wrong." She folded her arms and looked out the window.

"It's not like that," I said desperately.

"And you know what? When Cory Seymour asks how this could have happened, you're going to say that you don't stand for bullying. But guess what, Kate? You're *one of them*."

"I can't believe you'd say that to me," I said, tears filling my eyes.

"We're here!" the driver said happily, pulling into the driveway.

"You girls ready?" asked Dad, nervously turning his head back toward me and Haddie, not exactly eager to interrupt our best-friends-forever moment. "Kate? You . . . okay?"

"I'm fine," I said angrily, getting out and slamming the car door. "Let's just do this."

We walked toward the front of a massive white mansion. You could see mountains beyond the backyard, and, randomly, there was a school bus in the driveway.

"Hey," Haddie whispered, grabbing my wrist as we walked up a stony path to the ginormous front porch. "I'm . . . I'm sorry. That was stupid. I know you're not one of them. I just don't understand Taylor. But you're right. Maybe I should give her a chance."

Okay. This could work. This *was* working.

I gave her a smile, trying to ignore the rush of guilt settling in my stomach. "Thanks."

We stood anxiously at the door. Were we supposed to knock? Did he have one of those fancy doorbells that could see people? Or a security guard or something? Should we—

Suddenly the door swung open, and there he was. Cory Seymour, with blond hair and a faded gray T-shirt. A serious-looking guy stood next to him, and two people we recognized from his videos were tossing a football and laughing behind him.

"Oh my gosh! Kate the Great!" Cory said excitedly.

"*Wait,*" the man next to him said, holding out a sheet of paper to my dad. "Before we film a single second, we need this release signed. It states that we're allowed to film this interaction for Mr. Seymour's YouTube channel and advertise it in our promotional materials."

Dad looked over the sheet while Cory Seymour—*the* Cory Seymour, who'd interviewed celebrities and once jumped out of his window into his pool—gave me a hug.

"And wow—Haddie! When we heard you wanted to come, I was like, *yes.* Why didn't we think about it before?! This video will be killer. Legit inspiring and stuff. Right?"

"Um. Right," she said nervously. "Super inspiring. And stuff."

Dad signed the paper, apparently making Serious Guy happy, and Cory showed us into the mansion.

"Oh my gosh. Kate McAllister!" A girl with long, dark hair who was even taller than me ran up to us, clapping eagerly. "I'm so, *so* pumped! I sent that video to everyone I know. My little sister is in seventh grade, and the girls at her school are just the worst."

"This is Kendra, my assistant," said Cory.

"You girls need some water? Coffee, dude?" she asked my dad.

"Um, no thanks," he said.

"We'll take water, right, Kate?" asked Haddie. I knew what she was thinking—we were going to keep the empty water bottles till the end of time.

Cory showed us around the house. The main entryway's walls were made up of gigantic fish tanks. There was a trampoline in the middle of the living room. And the kitchen had an entire additional freezer just for ice cream. It was as if Cory had hired a little kid to design his dream house. I wanted to take photos for Taylor, but I also didn't want to look like a fangirl, even though I obviously was.

"All right," Cory finally said. "Let's do this thing, huh? Here's the main studio."

We walked into yet another giant room, this one with multiple cameras all pointing at a faded green couch. He flung himself onto it and kicked his feet up on the ottoman, motioning for us to join him. Two other guys adjusted some cameras, and Kendra was snapping a thousand photos on her phone.

"I'll just . . ." Dad motioned to the corner.

"Right! Sorry, dude. Wherever you're out of the way works great," Kendra said perkily.

Cory nodded at one of the guys, who flipped a camera on. No preparation, no sound check—we just dove right in.

"I am so honored to welcome to our show two girls

who have seriously impressed me this week. All the way from East Middle School in Madison, Wisconsin, Kate McAllister and Haddie Marks!"

So, what was the coolest part?

The coolest part was talking to someone I had watched on YouTube for years.

No, the coolest part was definitely when Kendra trotted out a ginormous check for the Wisconsin Anti-bullying Coalition.

Or maybe the coolest part was when we FaceTimed another twelve-year-old girl who was getting picked on at her school, and Haddie and I got to talk to her for a few minutes.

It might even have been that we left with autographed photos of Cory, and that he offered to hang out with us if we were ever in LA again.

But I think the coolest part was when Cory asked Haddie what she thought of having a best friend like me who was willing to risk her life to save Haddie's. And Haddie said, *I'm not even surprised. That's just who Kate is. She's not like other kids.*

That night, we needed hotel-room snacks. *Needed* them, we told Dad, and nothing in the vending machine would suffice. That type of need makes you feel like you'll never smile again if you don't get a Little Debbie snack, immediately. Those treats—like Zebra cakes or Swiss rolls—were the kind of food Mom always had the cabinet stuffed with. We were giddy and excited and could practically feel the blood flowing through our veins. Haddie and I were on top of the world. We were back in the rec center, that night of the thunderstorm, clutching those fireflies.

Dad called an Uber to take us to Walmart because it was the only place we knew that would be open that late. We had pulled on huge sweatshirts over our denim shorts.

"Girls. Don't go overboard. We have an early flight again," Dad warned as we pulled into the parking lot. "And it's been a long day."

"Sour Patch Kids, Zebra cakes, sour-cream-and-onion chips," Haddie said. "The trifecta of sleepover snacks."

"Perfected over years of experimenting," I explained to Dad.

"The perfect combo of sweet and salty," said Haddie.

"With just enough sustenance," I reminded her.

"Girls. Good Lord. Just get your snacks," said Dad.

We practically ran to the candy aisle, grabbing what we needed and then some. The store was playing the new Taylor Swift song extra loud, and we sang at the top of our lungs, making the tired, college-aged-looking kids in our aisle roll their eyes.

"You know," said Haddie, bopping me on the head with a Little Debbie box, "this really is the best sleepover we've ever had. Even better than when we snuck out to write on Mitchell Becker's driveway in chalk."

"Better than when my mom let us rent all three *Secret Scream* movies?" I asked, pointing a bag of Pixy Stix at her.

"Okay. Tied? Although I did have nightmares for weeks," said Haddie.

"I remember," I said, laughing. There is power in that—that simple *I remember*. It means so many things, to remember the same things as another person. Haddie knew the twists and turns of my very own story. I threw my arms around her, in the middle of Walmart, under the fluorescent light of eleven p.m.

"You're the one who saved *my* life, remember?" she joked.

"I missed you! I just . . . I've *missed* you." I laughed. She grinned.

"Girls!" Dad called. We scurried up to the cash register, Dad handing over his credit card and the cashier sleepily handing us our plastic bag of treasure.

Dad ordered another Uber to take us back to the hotel. As we climbed in, he asked the driver, "Could you take the long way so the girls can see some of LA?"

We drove up the highway, curving around and seeing the city of lights in the distance as we picked out all the red Sour Patch Kids. We asked the driver to open the sunroof and then stuck our heads out, our hair blowing in the wind, shrieking and laughing and making our Uber driver nuts. I grabbed Haddie's hand as our ponytails whipped around our faces. There she was: the friend I loved. And in that moment, we were Great—the both of us.

It's not like I planned to be out on our room's balcony at three a.m.

But you know the thing about Zebra cakes? That sugar makes it super hard to sleep. Even if you're on Wisconsin time and it's really five a.m. at home.

I stared at my phone, the text from Taylor I hadn't answered. When she finds out Haddie had come, she is going to be so mad. I felt bad—Taylor was my best friend.

But *best friend*: what did those words even mean? Not "friend I've known the longest," obviously. Not "friend I *trusted*." Not "friend who made me laugh." Someone to take selfies with? Someone to partner up with in lab? Someone to sit with at lunch? Was *Violet* one of my best friends? I didn't even like her.

I laughed out loud to myself. It felt so good to admit that, all of a sudden—that I didn't like Violet. Couldn't *stand* her. Amira was okay. Even Nico had his moments, like this one time in gym class, when Clara Quinn got assigned to his basketball team and he was so nice to her, giving her high fives even though she was kind of a geek and obviously the worst player. But Violet? If I never saw Violet again, I'd be happy.

What about Taylor? Did I like Taylor?

How could I not even know who I liked or didn't like?

But there was plenty I didn't know.

That day, by the pond. That hat. My hands.

Dad told me once that when he was interrogating people, the most important thing he did was listen to his gut. *The body knows, more than the head or the heart*, he said. *You listen to the body*. The truth, it could sit in your body, grow and expand like the cells we watched under a microscope in science. You could wish it away and go on fancy talk shows. Become a hashtag, whatever. But that truth, it does not leave. The heart pumps it out with every beat, and it burrows deep into your skin.

It had all happened so fast.

I just felt done, standing out there on the balcony. In

that moment, I was *done*, out, curtain call, final buzzer. I didn't want to be in Taylor's group anymore, the group of kids that thrived on the sorrow of others. That group of people who made themselves big by making other people small. I wanted to leave that club; I wanted my name off their list. I wanted to grab Haddie and run, run, run as far away from Taylor Tobitt as we could get. And that hat—

Landed—

My hands—

I was throwing it. *I wanted them to stop.*

I wanted it to stop, but I was not big enough to be the rescuer. I could not reach out and grab Haddie and shake sense into Taylor. I couldn't be the brave one. But I couldn't participate either. And that hat—it burned my hands. Before I knew it, I was throwing it, saw it soar through the air, and there it landed, in the middle of Woodglen Pond. Where it should have stayed.

Or had I? Had it been me, or *Violet*, yanking it? I could see Violet tossing it, but felt *my* hands doing it. I didn't know, I didn't know, I didn't—

Who had seen? Who *knew*? Clearly not Haddie. Taylor? Brett? It wasn't like I could ask.

Here's who didn't know: Maria Ramirez. Mustache Greg. Kendra. The girl Haddie and I had called today.

All these people hailing me as a hero, convincing me I was something big and important and special. Telling me that I was the person who made the Right Choice when she was faced with a tough question. But they were wrong, and I felt like that wrongness was surging through my entire body. I wasn't great—I wasn't anything but a liar.

My head was spinning. I had to sit down. I went back into our hotel room, shivering at the sudden burst of air-conditioning.

"Hey."

I jumped. "Geez, you scared me!"

Haddie was sitting upright on our bed. She was the last person I wanted to talk to right then—the person who deserved a good friend the most.

"I'm not the one who walked outside at three a.m.," she whispered.

"True," I said.

I climbed back into bed, and we both stared up at the ceiling. Maybe it's because it was pitch-dark in that room, with its fancy blackout curtains. Maybe it was because we really were messed up from all the sugar. Or maybe it was because Cory Seymour had called us brave. But I couldn't stop thinking about one thing in particular.

"Haddie?"

"Yeah?"

"Why didn't you rat on us—them—whatever. The people who were at the pond. Why didn't you tell Principal Howe what happened?"

She rolled over to face me. "I didn't want to ruin anyone's life."

I rolled over too. "You didn't want to ruin *my* life," I said.

She bit her lip. "You're my best friend."

Was I? Could I be?

"What was I supposed to say?" she whispered. "'The rest of those kids were jerks and then Kate saved me'? They would have made you look bad too. You would have gotten in huge trouble. And maybe . . . maybe everything that happened is for the best. Taylor and her friends have kind of laid off me. Are things going to be different when we get home? I mean, with you and me?"

I nodded. "Definitely."

"You don't use . . . that voice. Out here. That loud Taylor voice."

"Do I use a different voice at home?"

Haddie shrugged. "I used to always think Taylor had a certain voice. She'd talk, and it was kind of in a way to make everyone drop what they were doing and

160

listen to her? And then one day"—she bit her lip—"I tried to say hi at lunch?"

I knew what day she meant, instantly. It had been right around the time I'd stopped sitting with her. She had opened her mouth, hadn't even gotten a word out yet, and Violet had asked if she was there to say hi to *me*. Like she wanted to remind me that I didn't really fit in at their lunch table, and something about that ticked me off. Who was Violet to tell me where to sit? Who was she to try to act like I wasn't really their friend? So I'd snapped back, "No," and Haddie's face had fallen, so, so quickly.

"I remember," I said quietly.

"You used that Taylor voice, and I just . . . knew everything was different," she said. "But what I didn't know—what I *still* don't know is, why? Why are you friends with her?"

I didn't have to ask who she meant. Taylor, with her shiny blond hair. I remembered her putting her phone number in my cell that very first day of science. The feeling I got walking down the hall with her. Nobody could mess with me or make me feel smaller than I was. Nobody could talk about my weird mom who tried to sell everybody crap, or my police officer dad who pulled kids' parents over. My crumbling apartment when everyone else had nice houses with backyards. People *saw* me. I mattered.

"I guess . . . ," I whispered, "she made me feel chosen. Like she saw something special about me that nobody else saw."

Haddie rolled over and we lay in silence for a moment.

"Kate?" she whispered.

"Yeah?"

"I just want you to know," she whispered, "that I saw it first."

I SLEPT THE WHOLE WAY HOME FROM CALIFORNIA, THAT
uncomfortable airplane sleep where you dream about
the music playing through your headphones and keep
waking up with a sore neck. I just wanted to get home
and curl up on the couch. I didn't want to do another
interview, ever. Taylor texted me asking how it went,
and I couldn't even bring myself to text her back. What
was I supposed to do at school? Go to Taylor's lunch
table like nothing had happened? Switch back to being
Haddie's best friend? And how was I supposed to tell
Taylor about Haddie? Cory hadn't shared the video yet,
but he was going to as soon as it was edited. I needed
a plan, and fast.

When we landed in Madison, a little girl and her
mom ran up to me. "Kate the Great," they said excitedly,
asking me for my autograph. It's so weird how your
entire life can change but you're still the same you who

sleeps on a scratchy pullout couch and binge-watches Cory Seymour videos. Nothing about me had changed, except that *knowing*, that raw, aching feeling that the truth would not leave alone.

"Listen, Kate," Dad told me after the Uber driver dropped Haddie off. "I want things to go back to normal, okay? We've done a lot of interviews. Lots of fanfare. But you know this isn't going to last forever. Someone else is going to get their fifteen minutes soon. So let's chalk this up to a cool experience and return to the real world."

"I couldn't agree more," I said.

When we arrived at the apartment, I did my classic unpacking move—shoving everything into the laundry hamper—before collapsing onto my bed. It was only the early afternoon; I could have gone back to school, but Dad thought I needed sleep. He even called Coach Watt and told her I wouldn't be at basketball for the second day in a row, which I was pretty sure would send her into a coma. He went to work and I fell into a deep nap, the complete opposite of my airplane doze. When I woke up, I had a text from Mom.

So, so proud of you!!!! Dad said it went great.

So she'd talked to Dad, but not *me*?

I also had another text from Taylor: **???** 😒 I had no idea what that meant. I quickly clicked over to Cory

Seymour's channel, but the video still wasn't up. What was she asking?

I glanced at the time—dance practice would have just ended. I dialed Taylor and knew I was in for it as soon as she answered.

"Um, *hello*? Are you alive? You didn't text me back at all!"

Whew—just a text-ghosting freak-out.

"Sorry," I said. "I was so busy the whole time I was there. And then I fell asleep when I got home."

"Well?! Tell me *everything*! Did you, like, get a souvenir from his house? Wait, stop—I want to hear the whole story. Should I come over?"

"*No,*" I said instantly, probably louder than I should have. But I didn't want Taylor pedaling up to my mom's apartment on her bike to find it empty. "Um . . . let's do your house." Would telling Taylor in person about Haddie coming to California make things better or worse? "On my way."

When I got to Taylor's, she looked like she was about to explode, the way Watson gets when he hears the little *jingle-jingle* of his leash coming off its hook. "What took you so long? I just got a notification—new Cory Seymour video!"

Oh no. Oh no, no, *no*. This was not the plan—not this sudden ambush of truth after a big lie. Not Taylor dashing off into her big living room, the video already pulled up on her family's massive TV, not Stephanie in the kitchen, chopping strawberries. Not Taylor yanking me down on the sofa before I even had a chance to say anything, not her reaching for the Apple TV remote and hitting play, not—

Haddie and me, on that emerald couch.

Taylor looks at me and her eyes are wide. There's something: anger. Yeah. Lots of ticked-off anger. But also, under that anger:

Hurt.

She exhales, sharp and tight, but then—Cory Seymour starts talking, and so do I. "Taylor, I—"

She shakes her head and turns back to the TV. "I want to watch."

"You guys are just amazing," said Cory. "I mean, that level of bravery . . . normal people don't have that."

TV me smiled. "I guess it was just instincts."

"Well, a lot of people don't have 'being a good person' as an *instinct*. Selflessness is so rare, and what with the recent media attention that's been given to bullies, I think it's high time we gave some of it to heroes. And you, Kate the Great, are a hero."

Hero.

Villain.

What did these words even mean? Was Taylor really this evil, terrible person for making mean jokes? Was I really a saint for doing something I had read about in a magazine?

We were both, and neither.

"Wow," she said flatly when the video ended. "Cory Seymour called you a hero."

"Taylor . . ."

"I hope you and your bestie had a great time."

"Taylor. Stop. I'm sorry. I'm *really* sorry. They wanted to talk to her too. What was I supposed to do?"

"Um, *tell me*?" Fair point.

"I swear, I wanted to. I didn't know how. I—"

"Look, Kate. Let's get something clear here," she said. "I don't have time for people who don't want to be my friend. Okay? If you'd rather go be with Haddie, if you want to eat at her lunch table—"

"No! I don't!"

"It's just," said Taylor, biting her lip. "You're my best friend. And I feel like you don't even like being my friend anymore. Like you'd rather just go back to the way things were last year. Don't you like being in our group?"

"Of course I do," I insisted. And I did. Sometimes I really did.

I thought she'd stay mad. I thought she'd explode. But instead, Taylor just looked at me. "Okay, then," she said simply, as if she knew she'd won. "I thought that dress she wore was way too small for her, didn't you?"

A test. My heart was beating so hard I could feel it in my ears. To be a good friend to Taylor, I had to be a bad friend to Haddie. To be in Taylor's world, she had to be the center. *Oh, Haddie*, I thought, *I'm sorry. I wish I was the person everyone thinks I am.*

But I'm not.

"Totally," I said.

14

IN THE MORNING, THINGS SEEMED CALMER. I FEEL LIKE THAT'S usually the case. Big confessions can seem like small specks in the morning. Intense realizations, questions about who had a hat and who threw a hat—they can be brushed aside when the sun is out and you hear the garbage truck outside your window. I remembered Mom panicking at the end of the month, trying to hit her sales goals. After a night of sleep, she'd wake up with a game plan. *Here's what I'll do*, she'd say, drawing on her whiteboard. Making goals for sales parties and old high school friends and cold calls, doing the math, selling the lipstick. She always seemed to believe so strongly that it would work, even when it didn't, time and time again.

I'd gotten used to checking Mom's Instagram in the morning, but she'd barely been posting, which was weird. Now that she was surrounded by her True U buddies,

I'd expected tons of photos of group yoga sessions and makeover parties. The first few days had been one long Instagram story, but now, it was the occasional photo of a new eyeshadow palette or foundation and not much else. She'd shared my Cory Seymour clip, though, alongside a GIF of a girl jumping up and down with excitement.

School on Friday had been weird, but *everything* had felt weird since I'd saved Haddie's life. Haddie's mom had let her stay home from school to catch up on sleep, but I had no such luck—especially if I was going to play basketball for the state championships next weekend.

On Saturday morning, when I came into the kitchen, my dad was flipping pancakes and whistling to Ben Rector.

"Hey, Bird," he said. "Just in time. Chocolate chips or blueberries?"

"Do you have to ask?" I said, handing him a bag of Nestlé chips.

"Girl after my own heart."

Watson trotted up to me with his leash in his mouth.

"Dude. We just got back from a walk," Dad said. "I'm worried he's having self-esteem issues. All these walks?"

"He's going to become one of those fitness Instagrammers," I said. "Showing off his six-pack. Commenting on our calories."

"I'll have to buy him organic dog food from the health store," Dad said, mixing chocolate chips into the rest of the batter.

"What's the fancy breakfast occasion?" I asked.

"Long week. California, all that jazz . . . figured we could use a lazy morning with our phones turned off. Let someone else be on the news. Plus, you need fuel. Big game this afternoon."

"Maybe I'll call Mom. I haven't talked to her in, like, a week," I said.

Dad didn't say anything. I set the table and we chowed down, listening to Ben Rector sing about having an ordinary life. I felt it, in that moment: sweatpants and syrup and one of those warm spring days where we could leave the windows open.

"All the ice on the lake will be melted after today," said Dad. "No more saving people."

"Got it. I don't have time for heroics, anyway."

"Yeah, when do we need to leave for the game?"

"You're taking me?" I asked, surprised.

"Did you get your driver's license and forget to tell me?"

"Usually Houa's mom picks me up," I reminded him.

"I thought I'd drive you today. If you want. You're pretty used to riding around in the copper-mobile by now, right?"

"True," I said. "I guess I'll text her."

Dad took Watson for his second walk of the day, and I sat on the couch, dialing Mom.

"Hi, Katie lady."

I was surprised she had picked up. She sounded tired. *Exhausted*, like she needed a cup or seven of coffee.

"Hey, Mom."

"What's up?"

"I was just calling to say hi. Tell you about Cory and stuff."

"Yes! Give me just one second, I'm finishing an email . . . Okay. Hit me."

I gave her all the details and she did all the right Mom things, squealing when I said how big the hotel suite was and asking about which snacks we ate on the airplane. It made me think of the trips Mom and I had taken, riding on planes to go to True U conventions.

Even with chocolate chip pancakes and a reliable ride to basketball, what I really wanted right then was a lazy morning with Mom. One where we watched shows about girls picking out their wedding dresses and ate cereal for lunch. I felt tears poking behind my eyes.

"So . . . how's work going?"

"Good! *Good*," she said. But I recognized that voice. It was the one she gave Dad, or Haddie's mom, or our landlord. Or someone she was trying to recruit to be an Emerald Beauty Consultant. That Things-Are-So-Spectacular voice you use when things are anything but spectacular.

"Yeah? Are you getting close to Diamond?" I asked. She paused.

"Yes and no. You know what they say, Katie lady. The road to success is full of speed bumps." The True U Chief Empowerment Officer had said that on the Jamaica cruise, gesturing at the slideshow behind her and talking about how she'd been in six figures of debt when she started True U. I still remember how her curls didn't move when her head did, they were hairsprayed so tightly.

"So, not quite there yet?" I asked.

"Well." She cleared her throat. "I'm actually . . . I'm an Emerald. Right now. This month. But—"

"*What?*" She'd gone *backward*?

"It's just for this month. Nobody buys makeup in March. It's spring cleaning, clearing out your makeup drawers. And that Netflix show with the woman who organizes your house is totally killing sales, telling

173

people to live a more minimalist lifestyle. But she has that bright lipstick on! Total fraud, if you ask me."

"But—" The tears were starting to sneak out. Mom's True Emerald days had been tough. Home parties almost every single night and a lot of evenings where I sat and did homework, waiting for her to finally return. It had been kind of exciting, but it was stressful, too, since she had to buy a ton of product to have some on hand no matter what and she hadn't made any real money yet. It had been when she first started her business, when we were convinced she'd hit Diamond in four months.

"I'm going to bounce back! Aleena swears this happens all the time. I've seen it myself. You need to keep your eye on your dreams, Katie lady." I could hear her tapping her long fingernails. "I need to focus less on sales and more on recruitment. I passed my card to the Walgreens clerk today. She said she's been looking for a new job opportunity. Selling candy bars and toilet paper—who could blame her? So if I get her, plus another lady I met at the gym . . ."

"Mom. You said you were *so close* to Diamond. You said Utah was going to be the thing that got you there. And now . . . I mean, how are you even buying groceries?"

"That's not something you should be worrying about," Mom snapped. She was getting angry. "I'm the grown-up, Kate. You're the kid."

"You're not acting like one," I said, the tears starting to fall. "Why can't you just come *home*? You promised. You promised you'd go to Utah, become a Diamond, and come home."

"Sometimes life takes you in a different direction. But you follow the signs from the universe to go the way that's meant for *you*," she said.

"Mom! God! Stop talking in True U speak!"

"What's that supposed to mean?"

"Maybe you should just . . . come back and get a job," I said desperately. I'd thought it a million times, watching her draw on her whiteboard or pack up boxes of mascara, listening as people called one by one to say they couldn't make a home party. When all the other moms came to basketball team parties talking about their jobs as dentists or teachers or whatever. But I'd never said it.

Mom was silent.

"I mean, you're good at makeup. You could work at the counters in the mall. Or at Sephora," I said.

"Kate," she said quietly, "I *have* a real job. I'm a *business owner*." Mom cared so much about that. She always wrote it on forms, and there were times she *did* seem like a good leader. I'd seen her on team calls, excitedly walking her downline through their monthly goals, giving out prizes like lotion and under-eye concealer, reminding women that if they just dreamed big enough, they could do anything they wanted. Mom was good at inspiring people. Way better at it than makeup, to be honest.

"I don't think it's working, though," I mumbled through my tears.

"I need to go, Kate. You calm yourself down and call me later," she said. Silence. *Call Ended.*

I flung myself onto my bed and tried to stop sniffling.

Did she really not miss me at all? If True U wasn't going any better in Utah, why was she even *there*? Why couldn't she just get a real job? Anything other than trying to sell makeup on social media, talking all this rah-rah team garbage when really she was failing, failing, failing.

When Dad came home with Watson, he knocked on my door, but I yelled that I was taking a nap.

"It's nine a.m.," he responded.

"I'm resting before my game," I said.

And then I did take a nap, letting my eyes shut and drifting back to sleep. I dreamed of that ice breaking over and over again, but when I reached out, it wasn't Haddie. It was a thousand tubes of True U lipstick, spilling open, smudging my hands, turning them so red I would never be able to get them clean.

March meant tournament season for the East Middle Knights. Our district's own version of March Madness, and people took it seriously too. Our games were played at the high school we'd all eventually go to, in the gigantic field house. When Dad and I walked into the gym, there were already tons of parents in the bleachers, watching Elvejhem Middle completely cream Lowell. It smelled like popcorn and hot dogs, and you could barely hear yourself think over the squeak of basketball shoes and the *boing* of balls bouncing off rims.

I found my team quickly and dropped my purple gym bag by Alex and Houa.

"Look how tall their forward is," said Alex, tying her lucky maroon-and-gray shoelaces. "Like, six feet."

"We play them next week if we win today," said Houa. She tightened her ponytail.

Coach Watt pointed to me. "I usually wouldn't let someone play after they missed two practices the week before a tournament game. But I'm counting what you did as *service*, got it? You still need to be giving your all to this team." I nodded.

I sat to put my shoes on. Dad waved and went to talk to some other parents, who always called him "Officer," even though he had on an East Middle hoodie instead of his blues. He waved to Alex's brother, who he had gone to high school with. At home we had a picture of them together at prom, and my mom, too, with her big, giant belly under her shiny yellow dress.

I pulled on my basketball shoes and put my maroon bow in my ponytail. We all wore them. Taylor had texted that she would maybe swing by with Violet and Amira, but I didn't see them anywhere.

The game before ours ended, and Coach Watt waved us over while a few volunteers wiped down the floors and the other team slapped through their high-five line.

"All right, ladies. I'd like to see some hustle out there today. Sun Prairie has a couple of girls on their team who can run like lightning. Don't forget to pay attention to your pivots. Keep 'em focused. Starters: Houa, Shayla, Maya, Dawn, Kate. Knights on three."

We put our hands in, completely focused. If we lost today, it would be our final game of the year. I felt kind of barfy. We did our *One, two, three, Knights* chant, and our team jogged out onto the court.

Since I'm almost always taller than the other girl,

I do the opening tip. And that was true today. I stood across from a girl with dark braids who was at least a foot shorter than me. She didn't look happy about it.

The ref blew his whistle and threw the ball in the air, and I smacked it to Shayla, our point guard. The East parents cheered, and I heard Dad above them all: "Yeah, Bird!"

The game started off pretty well. Shayla dribbled down and passed it to Houa, who drove the ball up the baseline for a basket. The other team missed a couple of easy shots, and I was getting rebounds left and right. Coach subbed Alex and Rosa in for Maya and Dawn. I felt good, getting the ball, passing it to Shayla. I liked having just one job. I quickly learned the girl guarding me was named Stacey, since her coach kept screaming at her to put her hands up when defending me. Soon enough, they'd see I wasn't a shooter and send her to guard Dawn, but at the beginning, they're always clueless.

The first quarter was about half over when I heard it. *Kate the Great! Kate the Great!*

I looked up, and there they were—Taylor, Amira, and Violet, with a big sign. Sparkly maroon letters.

Suddenly, I could feel the parents whispering. *That's her? From* The Morning Buzz? *That tall one?*

"Head in the game, Kate," Coach Watt barked. I gave her a quick nod from the court.

Kate the Great!

The hat.

Kate the Great!

My hands—or Taylor's?—or—

Stacey leaped up after a failed three from Rosa, grabbing a rebound I should have easily gotten.

"It's all right, Kate. Just focus," said Coach, clapping and pointing at me.

We ran down to the other end. Stacey dribbled, passed to the girl from the opening tip, who put the ball up and—*swish*.

Coach pulled me out, putting Nikki in. I slumped into the bleachers, gulping down water from my bottle.

"Tell your friends to keep it down if you can't focus," said Coach. "In this gym, you're part of a team. Not a one-woman show."

I could feel my cheeks turning red, and not from being exhausted either.

"She sucks," Dawn muttered to me. I knew it was to make me feel better, but I turned away, embarrassed.

Brett had joined Taylor, Violet, and Amira. They sat up high in the bleachers, giggling and waving their sign. All eyes in the gym were on me now.

Coach put me back in a couple of minutes before half, but it was like my feet were stuck in the mud. Every time I got near the ball, Taylor would shriek, "Kate the Great!" And I'd do something stupid. I only got one rebound, and another time, I passed it to Houa when she was double-guarded. The ball felt like a thousand pounds in my hands.

At halftime, Coach gathered us around in a circle.

"We started strong, but they're gaining on us," she said. "Only up by four. Back to the basics, right? We need to keep everything else out of our heads. Dawn, you're at three fouls—if the girl's feet are set, you can't slam into her like that, right?"

We all nodded, but I wanted to sink into the gym floor. It was obvious who she was talking about. I glanced back at Dad, who shot me a thumbs-up.

"Why don't you just tell them to shut up?" Alex whispered to me.

"Because they're trying to be nice," I whispered back.

"They are?" she asked, confused. "It kinda seemed like they were trying to mess you up."

Wait . . . were they? It was so hard to tell with Taylor. Sometimes, when she wanted to be, she was your number one cheerleader. But other times, she was Taylor 2.0, the one who humiliated Haddie and didn't like it when anyone else shone brighter than her. But she always did it in this perfect way, so you couldn't *really* get mad. Like bringing a sign into a basketball game to supposedly cheer you on.

I looked at Alex, who raised an eyebrow at me. Then I looked away.

When halftime was over, Coach didn't put me in right away. But our team was tired. Sun Prairie caught up, their side of the auditorium exploding in screams.

"Kate. Alex. Claudia." Coach waved us over to go in.

Kate the Great!

Alex shot, missed. I leaped up and grabbed the ball, bringing it down securely. Threw it right back to her.

Kate the Great!

She tried again, missed again. The ball bounced off the rim. I jumped, caught it.

Kate the Great!

I was wide open as they double-guarded Dawn.

This time, I decided I would take the shot myself.

I never shoot. Ever. You'd think with my height I could just reach over and tap it in, but listen, I'm still bad at shooting. I set up my hands and—

Kate the Great!

Swish.

Our mojo was back. Braids Girl dribbled the ball in

and passed it to a short girl who shot and missed. Me with the rebound, to Alex, who hit a layup.

Taylor was quiet. Coach was clapping, yelling, "That's it, ladies! Kate, keep it up!"

It's not like I suddenly became Stephen Curry. But making that basket had put a little bit of pep in my step, and we went into the fourth quarter up by three. I rebounded over and over and over, tossing balls to Dawn and Houa, watching them sink baskets. Sun Prairie *was* super fast, with a couple of great shooters, so they put up a good fight. We ended up winning by eight—not exactly a knockout, but hey, we'd take it.

"Finals," Coach said, congratulating all of us after we finished our high-five line with the disappointed Sun Prairie Gophers. "We made it to the *finals*. And it's all because of your hard work. Great hustle out there today. Dawn with sixteen points, Houa with ten, and Kate—way to bounce back."

These were my favorite moments in basketball. When we *won*, and our team was together—hugging, shrieking, laughing, fixing each other's bows. I felt part of something so much bigger than what I really was, almost like when I was with Taylor's crew. But if I was being honest, a thousand times better. You could forget things when you were smiling for a victory picture, things like hats and Cory Seymour and lunch tables.

Dad bounded down the bleachers, wrapping me up in a big sweaty hug. "Bird! You were on fire out there!"

I looked up in the bleachers for my friends. But they had already left, taking their sign with them.

THIS SEEMS LIKE A HAPPY STORY, DOESN'T IT?

Girl saves friend. Girl scores basket. Girl is Great, a Hero, her Father's Daughter.

But we aren't done yet. Life is hiding around the corner, with something horrible up its sleeve.

After the game, most of the team went to Ella's Deli to celebrate. But I was exhausted, and whether it was from my phone call with Mom, California, the game, or realizing Taylor had only come to try to mess me up, I wasn't sure.

So Dad and I went home. He turned on college basketball and I took a long shower, reliving the moment I'd actually made a basket. After I got out, I was brushing my hair when my phone rang. It was Haddie.

"Hey," I said.

"Hey. How was your game?"

"It was good. We won, so we have state championships next weekend."

"Awesome," she said. "I was just going to see if you were coming on Friday."

"To what?"

"Um." She cleared her throat. "My birthday thing."

Oh my gosh. How could I have forgotten? I had spent every single March sixteenth at Haddie's house for dinner since I was six years old. It wasn't a big party, just her family, yummy food, and a movie we'd rent. Every single year, her dad would make a cake designed to look like whatever her favorite thing was that year. He was seriously good at it too. In second grade, he crafted a super-elaborate elephant cake, and last year, he made one to look like Haddie's favorite anime characters, with sparkles in their hair and everything. We always joked about signing him up for one of those baking competition shows.

"I mean—I know this year has been . . . weird. And stuff. But I feel like you not being there would be even weirder," she said quietly.

Weird was an understatement. It would definitely feel awkward to go. I had barely hung out with Haddie in months and hadn't been to her house since, like, October. Wouldn't her parents be annoyed with me? Or did they like me again, now that I had technically saved their kid's life?

Taylor would think the entire thing was babyish. For her birthday in December, Stephanie had dropped Taylor, me, Violet, and Amira off for pedicures at a spa.

But what about me? What about Kate the Great? What would *she* say?

Did I want to go to Haddie's birthday party?

"Yeah, I think so," I said. "I have to ask Dad. And I'll have a game the next day so I can't stay over too late . . ."

"Awesome!" she said excitedly. "I just didn't know if you were coming this year."

"Yeah. I guess I don't blame you. But I really want to."

"Want to just come over right after school Friday?"

"Sounds good. I'm excited."

"Me too," she said happily.

We hung up and Dad stuck his head into my room. "Hey, Bird. Who was that?"

"Haddie. She wanted to know if I'm going to her birthday dinner Friday."

"Is that a good idea, with your game the next day?"

"I'll just go for a little bit."

"We really need to get this room fixed up," he said, glancing around. "I know I keep saying that. But we should put a new coat of paint on. Get you a real bed."

"I might be here for a while," I said, remembering

my morning conversation with Mom. "I talked to Mom today." It all came rushing back, and before I could even tell him about the conversation, I was blinking back a few tears.

Dad sighed. "She upset you, didn't she? Of course she did. It's Casey. I wish she'd just grow up. I'm sorry you have to deal with this, Bird. It's not fair."

That ticked me off. Once again, I was playing defense—making sure Dad didn't take any shots on Mom, making sure Mom got the rebound.

Mom was far from perfect. But she had been all I'd had, for a long time.

"*No*. She didn't upset me at all," I said. "In fact, she's doing great."

Dad looked surprised. "She *is*?"

"Yes," I lied. "She made it to Diamond status."

It just popped out. I mean, it wasn't so much of a *lie* as it was me getting ahead of myself. Mom would work her way back up the True U chain any day now.

He froze. "Is that . . . what she told you?"

"Yes. She might have to stay in Utah longer, because things are going so well. It would be hard to come back after she's gotten so ingrained in the True U community. So I might be here for a while. That's all I'm saying."

I was hoping for a nod of approval, for an *oh wow*

188

look. A sign that he took Mom seriously. But instead, Dad just looked confused.

"Kate, you know you can be here as long as you need, right?"

"Yeah. Sorry you're stuck with me."

"Pretty sure it's the other way around," he said with a half smile.

"I'm going to bed," I said.

"Already? It's not even nine. Although, the game, right? You're probably pooped."

"Yeah."

"Hey . . . Bird? Can I ask you something?"

"Sure."

"Taylor and her crew today. Did they—were they trying to be funny, or . . . what was that about?"

I shrugged. "I don't know."

"Okay," he said. "Just checking. Because, you know . . . seventh grade . . . it's tough. Your mom had these mean girls in her class—"

"She did?" I asked, surprised. Mom had never told me that.

"Oh man, yeah. Lisa Girard. She got everyone to call your mom Space Case because she would daydream in class a lot. I still remember how mad your mom would get."

"That's the dumbest attempt at an insult I've ever heard," I said flatly. Say what you would about Taylor, but she was a lot wittier than that.

He laughed. "I know. So stupid. Ask her about it sometime. But I guess what I'm saying is that if there are some kids being jerks, make sure you're standing up for yourself. Your mom sure did."

"Dad," I said, "Taylor isn't Lisa Girard. She's my best friend."

He held his hands up. "Okay, okay! Just making sure. Sometimes it's hard to tell."

He said good night and went into the living room to watch more basketball, and I pulled up my email. But what I really needed was Mom herself: there, telling me everything was going to be okay, telling me she was going to back any minute. But that's not what I had. So I went to sleep.

16

SUNDAY MORNINGS AT DAD'S MEANT CHURCH. MOM LIKED God okay, but she wasn't a big churchgoer. She'd pray out loud when she was looking for a parking spot, and she had a whole cupboard full of rosaries, which she said you weren't supposed to throw away. But I think actual church buildings made her kind of itchy.

Dad, however, went to church. Period. Once I told Dad that Mom had said she felt God more on a walk outside than she did in a building. He said it was wonderful that she felt God out in nature, and that we should go thank him for that presence by going to church.

So. Sunday mornings when I was at Dad's, which was apparently going to be a lot more, I had to look somewhat put-together by eight forty-five so we could zip over to Sacred Heart. I really did like Dad's church. It was homey: think more cozy-living-room and less coronation-of-a-fancy-king. It had huge stained-glass windows and wood-paneled walls, always giving it this clean, brightly lit feel. The priest, Father Andrew, used to be a pediatrician, so he was really good with little kids and never got mad when they cried during his sermons.

"Kate?"

There was Taylor, in a cute white dress with gold sandals. She always put together the best outfits. Church clothes for me meant this pleated skirt Mom had bought me last year for my great-uncle's funeral.

"Hi," I said.

"I didn't know you were at your dad's this weekend," she said.

Oh yeah.

I still hadn't *exactly* told my best friend that I'd moved in with my dad.

I didn't really know why. It was something about seeing Taylor's house, with its huge TV in the basement, and the way she always had a fridge stocked with soda. Taylor's house was so perfect. Her *life* was so perfect. And I lived in an apartment building. I didn't even have a real bedroom. It's not like Mom's place had been that great either—I'd seen the look cross over Taylor's face when I explained we had students living upstairs. But something about an apartment building just felt even weirder. And besides, where was I supposed to say Mom went?

"Yeah," I said, glad that my dad was chatting with some other parishioners. "I forgot you guys go here sometimes."

Taylor rolled her eyes. "Only when Stephanie's in a phase. Hey, what are you doing this afternoon? Want to come over or something?"

"Sure. I'll ask my dad," I said.

"Good. Didn't know if you were too famous for me now," she said, laughing. That not-funny laugh again.

"*Stop*," I said. "You know someone else will get their fifteen minutes next week. That's what Dad keeps saying."

"He's probably right," she said, checking her hair for split ends. "I mean, no offense, but it's not like it was *that* big of a thing. A joke got out of hand and she fell in some cold water. Like, must have been a slow news week."

"Totally," I mumbled.

"So, this afternoon? Cory Seymour dropped a new video. I'll wait to watch it with you, if you want."

"Sounds good," I said, then headed back to Dad. I slid in next to him in the pew, and he opened his mouth. Shut it. Opened it again.

"Dad, *what*?"

"Does Taylor not know you moved in with me?"

Oops. I guess he hadn't been as distracted as I'd thought.

"Not exactly."

"Why? Are you—are you, like, embarrassed?"

"It's not like I lied to her. I just haven't mentioned it."

"You haven't mentioned to your best friend that you moved?"

"It's temporary," I bit back. "I don't even have a bedroom."

Ouch. That hurt. I felt bad right away, but the cantor started singing, and Father Andrew was following the altar servers down the aisle. I turned to look forward. But not before I caught a glimpse of my dad's sad face.

After church, Dad had to run some errands. I finished up my homework before heading to Taylor's on my bike. It was actually pretty boring—we watched the new Cory Seymour, and then I sat there while she scrolled through Instagram and talked about Violet's new highlights, which apparently made her hair look super fake. My dad would never let me dye my hair in a billion years, so I just nodded along. I felt bad, sitting there, talking about Violet like that. Violet and Taylor had been best friends since kindergarten. She had a photo of her and Taylor as her phone background. Taylor had one of herself and me.

"Aren't you *so* excited for things to go back to normal?" she asked, turning her phone to show me that Cory had posted a photo with me and Haddie.

"I guess," I said.

"I mean, having to pretend to be Haddie's friend?" She shuddered.

Haddie and I, on the plane, in the hotel, laughing through the grocery store. My heart thudded. Operation Get Haddie and Taylor to Be Friends was supposed to be in full swing by now. Time for action.

"You know," I said cautiously, "Haddie can actually be kind of fun."

Taylor froze, dropped her phone, and looked at me. "What?" she said.

"I just mean . . . I was friends with her for a long time. So I know her pretty well. And she's really funny. She—she's a good listener, too, and—"

"*Wow*," said Taylor, laughing. That mean laugh. That *knife* laugh. "Someone's got a new bestie, huh?"

I felt my face get hot. "What's your *problem* today?"

"What's *my* problem? I don't have a problem. *You're* the one who decided to go be best friends with Haddie

Marks." She said her name like you'd say *Watson's poop.*

"I'm not—we're *not* best friends," I said. "You're my best friend."

"Doesn't sound like it. I'm not the one you took to California."

"I told you, I should have let you know earlier . . ." *Why?* What was I even saying sorry for? It was like Taylor could make you doubt your own thoughts.

"Why don't you just leave?" she asked. All jokes were gone. Her eyes were angry. "Go see if Haddie's free. I'll call Violet—"

No. No. This was not going according to plan.

"We're *not friends.* I was *kidding,*" I said.

We sat in silence.

I hadn't been kidding. She knew that. But to cover something up with a joke so the other person can't get mad? That was a Taylor Tobitt trick. I could do it too.

"Fine," she said flatly. "Just don't forget it."

Why are you even friends with her? Haddie and Dad. Both asking the same question. Why was I even friends with Taylor? Because the power that came with walking down the hallway next to Taylor, the way I felt when I had a seat at her lunch table, the envy in everyone's eyes when she passed *me* a note in English— sometimes, it felt like all I had. It didn't matter how many stickers of the True U motto Mom plastered around the house. I'd never had a spotlight to step into. But I was Taylor Tobitt's best friend, and I wasn't ready to give that up just yet.

"Do you still want to hang out?" I asked. I felt kind of teary.

She sighed. "I should get some homework done." She glanced out the window. "What are you doing this week?"

"Basketball practice. But we don't have any on Friday so that we're rested for Saturday. Our championship game."

"Did you love our sign?" she asked.

"Totally," I said.

"Since you don't have practice, want to go to Ella's Deli with Violet, Amira, and me Friday night for ice cream? Violet's mom can take us."

Did they already have a plan? Was this a pity invite? Why hadn't they invited me in the first place?

"You sure?" I asked, trying to sound casual. "Sounds like you have it all planned out . . ."

Taylor just shrugged. "Violet asked us to go. But she won't care if you come."

Yeah. Sure she wouldn't.

"Sounds good," I said. "I'm in."

"Cool. We'll walk to Violet's after school and go from there," she said.

"Okay."

"Hopefully your celebrity status will have faded by then," she said, rolling her perfectly mascaraed eyes. "Because I seriously can't handle any more Haddie Marks talk."

When I got home late that afternoon, Dad was waiting for me. He was bouncing on the heels of his feet, looking like Dawn waiting for the referee to wave her into a game.

"Um, hi?"

"Bird. Big surprise."

"Please tell me it doesn't involve shiitake mushrooms." The last big surprise had involved a purchased wok and a weekend of dinners that caught on fire.

"Come see," he said, pushing open the door to the office.

When I stepped inside, I couldn't believe it.

A bed. A *real* bed, with a thick blue comforter the color of the sky. A mountain of pillows. The desk was gone, and so were the signed Aaron Rodgers poster and Creepy Jesus. There was a dresser, white with gold handles and a few framed photos on top—Dad and me, my basketball team portrait, me and Haddie in fourth grade, licking Popsicles and sticking out bright green tongues. One with me and Mom, too, our faces pressed close together, our eyes happy. It was nice of him to pick that one.

"What . . ."

"It's time to give you a real room," Dad said proudly. "I did all this myself."

"You bought me a bed?!"

"Well. Technically it's a hand-me-down. But the guy who sold it to me is on the squad, so he helped me haul it up here. The dresser's just from Ikea but it took me an hour to put together, so you better like it. I'm sorry I didn't let you pick one out, but I wanted it to be a surprise. I thought I could give you your birthday present three months early and you and Taylor or Haddie or whoever could browse for some posters online. I can give you my credit card. Fifty dollars tops, though, okay? Don't go nuts."

"Dad . . ." I looked around the room.

"We can paint too. Not right now, since things are so busy with the news and with work, and your basketball tournament . . . but eventually? You can pick the color. Whatever you want."

"Where will you do your paperwork?"

"The kitchen. My own room. Whatever," he said, waving a hand.

The room was perfect, somehow. It might not have been the colors I would have picked, and the photo of me and Haddie was kind of old. But still. There was a bedside table that matched the bed with a white lamp on it, and the lampshade matched the comforter perfectly. Like he'd gone to Target and bought a set, which he probably had. That lamp, sitting there, felt so . . . intentional. I could see him in the housewares aisle, trying to figure out which color I'd like best, making sure I had light to read.

Who knew a lamp could make you want to cry?

I turned and hugged him, hard.

"I didn't mean what I said," I said. "At church. I feel bad . . ."

"It's okay. I'm just—I'm happy to have you here. I want you to feel like you're at *home* while you're here. These past few weeks have been hard. I know that. But having you living with me has been some of the happiest times of my life, and it may be selfish, but I hope you'll stay for a while."

"But I was mean, about the room. It didn't even bother me, sleeping in the office."

"Kate. That's not why I did this. You need a real bedroom."

The truth was, I'd *never* really had a room that felt like mine. With Mom there was always a new place to live—a townhouse that had a yard and always smelled like the Korean barbecue next door, an apartment that was closer to downtown but also meant students keeping us up all night, one where they said we could paint the walls any color we wanted so we stayed up all night painting the kitchen a lemony yellow. My room was always filled with things that weren't mine, because we didn't have a lot of space—the huge boxes of True U sales brochures Mom insisted on lugging from place to place, her extra makeup brushes, packages we had to return. I'd see rooms in catalogs or on TV and dream about having one that really felt like *me*, but I never got it.

Somehow, in this stupid apartment building with its hotel floors and fire escape, I had one. It wasn't perfect. It didn't look like a magazine. It didn't have a gigantic TV on the wall, or a fireplace, like Taylor's. But it was mine. And that made it perfect.

17

THERE WERE A FEW BIG DIFFERENCES BETWEEN LIVING WITH
Mom vs. Dad that I was still getting used to.

The first was nighttime. I was used to staying up
pretty late. Mom usually boxed orders or did Instagram
shoots at night, and I would hang out in the kitchen
with her, doing homework or bingeing YouTube. Or
just talking to her. We'd talk and talk, and she'd tell
me stories about when she was a little kid and lived in
Chicago before moving to Madison, how her grandpa
was an artist who drew for kids' picture books. I'd
tell her about some dumb thing I'd done with Taylor,
and she'd ask my advice on her Instagram shots. We'd
laugh so hard we couldn't catch our breath when I'd
tell stories about Principal Howe's saliva issue, or she'd
tell me about the time she and her sister stole all her
mom's makeup and created a mural on the kitchen
wall with lipstick and eyeliner. We'd glance at the clock

and be surprised it was one a.m., and she'd practically shove me into bed. I'd be tired the next day, but those late nights were worth it a billion times over in my mind. When Dad went to bed, he expected me to go to bed too. I got it—he had to be up driving a police car around and solving real issues in the morning. But I wasn't used to a quiet home by eight thirty. I tried to tell Dad a story about Taylor one night, and he kind of chuckled, but it wasn't the same. Mom would have dissected every ounce of the Taylor-basketball-sign saga and helped me make a game plan for what to do. She would have helped with Operation Get Haddie and Taylor to Be Friends, like my coconspirator. Dad . . . I didn't know if he would get it.

Another was having a dog. Mom and I had never had a pet because we were usually renting somewhere that didn't allow them, but Dad's apartment building was cool with it as long as they were small. So I was getting used to Watson. Yeah, he had to be taken out a lot, and okay, he barked. But he was also a snuggler. And something just felt right about curling up in bed at the end of the day with a pile of fluff snuggling up next to me. The way he'd trot over to me and promptly fall on his back for a belly rub was pretty cute too. I could see why Dad had adopted him, even though I'd had to pick way too much dog hair off my sweatshirts. I wanted to start babysitting this summer, or running errands for Mrs. Levine, to save up enough money to get Dad one of those robot vacuums for Christmas so that Watson's hair wasn't on every single inch of carpet.

But one of the *biggest* differences? Grocery shopping.

Going to the store with Mom was an art form. We'd meal-plan for the week, browsing through the coupons that came in the mail and checking the store's app to see what was on sale. I knew that chickpeas were cheaper than meat, and pasta was super filling, and a big bag of frozen broccoli could go a long way. I didn't qualify for free lunch at school because of Dad's child support every month, which I knew stressed Mom out, but honestly, I was kind of happy about it. I couldn't imagine Taylor, with her Kate Spade backpack, finding out that we were calculating the pears vs. peaches price difference.

Then, we'd go to the store and track the price of everything on our phones as we put it into the cart. Mom would get super excited if stuff was on an even bigger sale, or if we found the *Woohoo* stickers. They were these little stickers they'd put on stuff that meant it was an extra-deep discount. Entire things of sandwich meat for a dollar, that kind of stuff. Mom would give a real-live *woohoo*, which was embarrassing, but I do have to admit, I felt pretty victorious when our grocery bill was lower than expected. It was a game—and we were varsity-level.

Going to the store with Dad was the opposite.

Chocolate sauce so we can make ice cream sundaes? Yeah, whatever, throw it in the cart. Chicken's on sale? Great, but that means we better stock up and freeze it. Carrots are annoying to cut up; let's buy the pre-sliced ones. I'd always thought of *rich* as someone with a mansion and a reality show, or even Taylor, with her own TV in her room. But I was starting to think of *rich* as a person who doesn't have to look at the price of an avocado before they buy it.

Money in general was just different with Dad. He didn't have a ton, but he definitely had more than Mom. He just paid for stuff without really thinking about it. I think the reason he could do that was probably because he didn't go on vacations and didn't buy anything fancy. But choosing the juice that was already made in a bottle instead of the package of concentrate without thinking twice might as well have been a trip to Hawaii for Mom and me.

The problem with Dad's strategy was that shopping took forever, since he wasn't exactly going in with a plan. So he'd sent me back to produce to grab apples ("Which ones?" "Doesn't matter. Just some I can take to work and munch on." "But, like, Red Delicious? Granny Smith?" "Kate. Apples. Round and red."), and as I was standing there, debating between Cortland and Honeycrisp, I heard my name.

"Kate!"

I turned and saw Houa's mom, weighing some Brussels sprouts.

"Hey, Mrs. Khang," I said.

"Ready for next weekend? You were on fire yesterday," she said.

I grinned. "Well. Rough start."

She waved a hand. "Please, that's sports. You girls pulled it off, and that's what matters. I already told Coach Watt that if you win the championship, the after-party can be at our house."

"Sweet!" I loved the Khangs' house. They had a huge basement with a pool table and a trampoline in the backyard.

"Are you with your mom? I ran into her the other day at Target."

I froze. *What?*

Maybe Mrs. Khang was one of those people who said *the other day* but meant *two months ago*. Haddie would sometimes tell a story like it had happened the day before when really it had been last year.

"Target?" I asked.

"Yeah. Yesterday morning, before the game. I had to get Houa some Band-Aids for her feet. The girl's heels are ripped to shreds from those new shoes she just had to have."

I shook my head, slowly. "My mom's in Utah. She moved there, actually." Who knew why I was telling my basketball teammate's mom when I hadn't even told my best friend, but out it came. "I live with my dad right now."

"Oh!" She looked surprised. "So is she just in town for a bit, then? I wish I had known; I asked if I would see her at the game."

Mrs. Khang had always been so nice to my mom. Once, she hosted a True U party for her and invited all four of her sisters. Those kind women, nibbling on chocolate chip cookies, letting my mom smear foundation onto their faces. Mom had even recruited one of Houa's aunts to her team of sellers, but I think she quit after a few weeks.

"I— She's not in town. She's in *Utah*," I repeated.

Mrs. Khang looked confused. "Oh."

"Yeah."

We stared at each other, neither of us knowing what to say. Clearly, we thought the other person had spent too much time inhaling the smell of produce.

"All right," she said awkwardly. "Well. So good running into you. I'll tell Houa I saw you."

"Yeah. Tell her I'll see her tomorrow," I said.

"Yup," she said, fake-cheerfully, wheeling her cart away from the loony toon with the apples.

She was the loony tune. Mom was obviously in Salt Lake City. Who had Mrs. Khang seen? A Mom lookalike? Unless—

"Oh my gosh . . . are you that girl on TV?" A tall woman put her hand on my shoulder. "Kate something? Kate the Great! From *The Morning Buzz*!"

I gave a half smile. "That's me."

"I have to take a picture with you. My husband's never going to believe this! This is so cool." She held out her phone for a selfie and I smiled awkwardly.

"Excuse me? What are you doing?" It was Dad, but with his cop voice.

"I just— It's Kate the Great! I've never met a famous person before . . ."

"She's not famous," said Dad angrily. "She's twelve. You can't just grab people and take photos with them."

"Dad—"

"Kate, I've been waiting for you. Let's check out. Now."

"Sorry," the woman mumbled as Dad yanked me away.

"*Dad.* Don't do the cop thing!" This happened often— Dad's cop voice. Officer McAllister might not be driving around town, but he would pop out when you least expected him to, like he'd just been hiding behind a curtain.

"First of all, she doesn't even know that I'm a cop," he said. "I'm in plainclothes. Secondly, Kate, have I taught you nothing? Random photos with people? I thought we were trying to let this all die down."

"It is! I didn't do anything! *She* grabbed *me*."

"Well, you should have said no. No more photos, no more interviews, no more *nothing*, okay? I want you focused on kid stuff. Your friends and your homework and basketball."

"I'm *not* a kid," I snapped back.

"Last I checked, twelve? Can't vote, can't drink, can't drive."

We got to the checkout line and the cashier stared at us a moment too long, clearly trying to figure out if he knew me from somewhere.

"Paper bag," Dad snapped, even though he hadn't been asked.

"Dad," I whispered, mortified. The cashier quickly checked us out, even more embarrassed than I was, and we hurried to the car.

As we drove home, it started to rain. It was one of those cold spring rains that make everyone miserable. Dad flicked on the windshield wipers.

"Kate, I'm sorry. I didn't mean to lose it on you. It's just . . . these days, I don't think people think enough about privacy. That woman was probably going to put that photo on social media. Then people would maybe see a sign in the background. Know where you grocery shop. Maybe you inspired this person, sure, but maybe someone else, you ticked off. Or maybe someone else is just straight-up unstable. *Violent.* You think I'm being dramatic? I see this kind of stuff happen every single day. There are some things we don't put on the internet. And random pictures with strangers is one of them."

"Okay, Dad." I pulled out my phone and brought up Mom's Instagram.

Mrs. Khang must have seen someone who looked just like her, because her bio still said *#GirlBoss + mama living in SLC to pursue my DREAMS. Ask me about our NEW True-ly Tantalizing Lash Boost!* There she was, smiling with Aleena, holding up a mascara.

And then. Her most recent photo.

She was holding a glass of wine, and she looked tired. I'd seen my mom do a million True U pitches, and I could tell when her heart was in it and when it just wasn't. When months were hard, or she lost some True Emeralds on her downline, or she just missed an important goal. When, last year, she didn't rank high enough to be invited on the Totally True Bahamas Cruise. Her eyes looked sad, even though she was smiling.

The caption was covered in emojis, talking about big life changes and the road to success not being straightforward. She ended it by encouraging people to *Take the LEAP into your DREAM LIFE. Why not U? Step into your SPOTLIGHT!*

But that wasn't what caught my eye.

It was the background.

It could have been anywhere. It was a brick wall— they have those in every city in the US. But in the corner, as if it had been pushed to the side, you could just barely see the curve of a chair. Not just any chair.

A University of Wisconsin *terrace* chair.

A type of chair that you famously cannot buy any- where else and cannot replicate.

This photo was taken in Madison. On campus. A few miles from the Windy Willow Brook apartment complex.

Dad pulled into the parking lot and shut the car off. "Ready, Bird? Hey, what are you looking at?"

I turned the phone to show him, and then I saw the look on his face. It was not one of *Surprise!* Or *Oh my gosh!*

It was one of *Oh crap.*

And he was looking at me.

He knew.

"Kate . . ."

"Mom's *here*? Mom's in *Madison*?"

"Kate. Okay. Listen to me for a sec."

"What is she *doing* here?! Why didn't she call me?"

Dad sighed, rubbed his chin with his hand. "Her job . . . it's not going great. She's having a hard time. She thought maybe if she came back here, stayed with Jess—"

"She's—she's staying with who? *What*? How long has she been here?"

"Jess? I don't even know. An old friend, I think. Someone who's letting her crash. She's low on money . . . It's complicated, Kate. These things are so complicated. Ah man."

"How. Long."

Dad looked at me, and I swear, I saw his eyes get teary. "Maybe like . . . a week?"

"Wow. Okay, so—you *lied*. You guys lied to me. I

can't *believe*—" Now I was crying, and breathing fast. I felt like I was in a basketball game and the buzzer was about to go off.

"Kate, come on. Let's go inside and talk about it. Okay? Get out of this rain, huh?"

"I am not going *anywhere* with you." I jumped out of the car, slamming the door behind me as hard as I could. Then, in the rain, I grabbed my bike from where it had been chained to the parking lot rack and took off.

"Kate! *Katherine Louise McAllister!*"

But I was gone. Gone like my mother, gone like the dreams she'd dashed, gone like any faith I had that my parents could be normal, gone like any hopes of standing up to Taylor. Washed away in the rain.

I DON'T KNOW WHY I DECIDED TO GO TO HADDIE'S HOUSE. I kind of panicked. *Rational* and *angry* don't really mix. In my life, when I'm mad—that fiery, seething mad that grabs hold of my throat and feels like it's going to choke me—I don't actively decide things. I just do them. I just wound up on Winnequah Court, knocking at 205, hoping someone was home.

Juliet answered. Haddie's mom—I *loved* Haddie's mom. She was everything my mom wasn't. She had long brown hair that she never styled, but instead put in a tight bun every single day, and she wore these round glasses. She was wearing a beige sweater, the color of a potato.

"Kate!" She was surprised. Obviously. I was soaking wet, my jeans sticking to my legs. My ponytail was matted to the back of my neck.

"Hi, Juliet," I said.

"Come on in." She opened the door wider and I stepped in, dripping a puddle on their mudroom floor.

"Sorry about the mess. Is, um . . . is Haddie here?"

"She is. Haddie!" But she didn't have to yell. Haddie bounded down the steps, having heard me walk in.

"Kate! Oh my gosh, did you ride your *bike* here? Are you out of your mind?"

"Sorry," I said. "I'm sorry. I . . ." I felt like I was going to cry, my puddle now turning into a small pond right there in the entryway. It was so stupid. But I hadn't known where else to go.

"Are you okay, Kate?" Juliet asked me, looking kind of worried. "Does your mom know you're here?"

"She's in Utah, Mom. Kate's at her dad's," Haddie said.

"No," I said. "No, she's not. She's in Madison. It's a long story. I'm about to text my dad. I just wanted to see if you wanted to, like, hang out. I didn't mean to invite myself over, but—"

"No! Oh my God. Don't worry about that," Haddie said.

"You know you're always welcome here, Kate," Juliet said, giving my shoulder a squeeze. "Especially after what happened a couple of weeks ago. I can't believe I haven't really gotten a chance to see you since then. Talk to you. I mean . . . *thank* you, really."

I just nodded awkwardly. "It wasn't that big a deal." Then I realized how dumb that sounded. Because, *duh*. It was her kid. Of course it was a big deal.

"It was to me," Juliet said kindly. "You girls go upstairs. Haddie can lend you something to wear. Do text your dad, though, okay? Or is he working?"

"I'll text him," I promised.

"Good. I'm just finishing up some work in the office, and there's some potato soup in the Crock-Pot for dinner. Rainy Sunday like this, we need soup."

Haddie and I went upstairs, and she lent me some sweatpants and her Ravenclaw T-shirt. I opened my phone to find four missed calls, all from Dad. I shot him a quick text: **Really mad at you. Went to Haddie's. Be home later.** And he responded: **OK. Please be home by 7 so we can eat dinner together + talk. Let me know if I should come get you in the car. I ♥ you ◍.**

I hadn't been in Haddie's room since October, even though I'd spent almost every single summer morning here, watching YouTube and making bracelets and planning how seventh grade would be the best year of our lives. It looked pretty much exactly how I remembered it. There was even still a picture of me and her, in sleeping bags, smiling in the rec center. "I just can't get over the fact that she's here, and didn't even want

216

to see me," I said. "It's like . . . she doesn't miss me at all." After I got changed, we stretched out on the floor of Haddie's bedroom, eating pickle popcorn from Trader Joe's, one of our all-time favorite comfort foods.

"I'm sure that's not true," Haddie said right away. "Maybe she's just embarrassed. You know, if her business isn't doing too good or whatever . . ."

"Too embarrassed to talk to *me*? I've been there through every stupid True U thing," I argued. And she *lied* to me. Just straight up said she was in Utah for a while, wasn't coming back anytime soon . . . She's right here! Staying at some friend's apartment. Drinking wine at the campus *terrace*."

"That's so . . . ugh," she said, shaking her head. "I can't believe she'd do that."

"I *know*. She didn't even try to come to my basketball game or anything! I'm just off living with my dad, la-di-dah, while she does *whatever*. And her business is tanking, so who knows when she's going to figure her crap out." I shoved a handful of popcorn in my mouth.

"Well, maybe . . . I don't know. Maybe she thought it would be best for you to be somewhere not so intense right now. Your dad doesn't move as much, right?"

"Yeah, but come *on*. She couldn't have told me that?"

Suddenly, there was a knock on the bedroom door.

Haddie's older sister, Natalie, poked her head through. Natalie was a senior at East High, though she was about to be a freshman at Northwestern in the fall. I'd seen it on Instagram. She had on a Northwestern Wildcats hoodie and her long dark hair was in a braid.

"Hi, Natalie!" I said excitedly. I'd always loved Natalie. I'd actually missed her a ton the past few months. She was super smart, and she was also always in the high school musicals. Haddie and I had seen her star as Dolly in *Hello, Dolly!* three times last year. She'd even been prom queen as a junior, and everyone just thought she was so . . . nice. She was pretty much the epitome of everything you'd want to be when you were a senior in high school. Popular, but not like Taylor. People wanted to be around her because they *liked* her, not because they were kind of afraid of her.

"Hi," she said.

But not a *Hi, Kate! How are you? Long time no see!* Like Juliet had given me.

This was a *Hi, person I don't really want to talk to.*

And everyone in the room knew it.

I looked down at the ground, but not before I saw Haddie shoot Natalie a look. Natalie didn't seem to care, though—she just stared at me.

"Just seeing what you guys were up to," she said.

"Nothing," said Haddie.

Here's the thing about being someone's best friend for seven years: you know what their *nothing* means. You have a shared history. You speak their language fluently. There's a different *nothing* for when your mom asks you what you did at a sleepover or what sounds good for lunch. And then there's the *nothing* you use when your sister is pissing you off. What I'm saying is this: there was a whole conversation happening in that room, but none of it was said out loud.

"Okay. Great." It wasn't great. Natalie looked at Haddie, then back to me. "So, like, what's Kate doing here?"

"Hanging out," Haddie mumbled.

"Hanging out?" Natalie laughed.

"Nat . . . ," said Haddie.

"I'm just saying," said Natalie. "It's kind of weird that you're here, Kate, isn't it? After you haven't been here for months? And then you guys just, what? Decide to be best friends again?"

"We're still best friends," said Haddie.

"Haddie." Natalie rolled her eyes. "How many nights were you crying that Kate didn't like you anymore? That Kate had ditched you? That Kate's friends were bullying you? I know that's why you were out on that ice. I wouldn't be surprised if Kate herself had something to do with it."

My eyes filled with tears. It was all just too much. My kind-of fight with Taylor, the news about my mom, the bike ride in the rain, Natalie's angry eyes. I'd known Natalie since she was in sixth grade. I was there when she won the statewide spelling bee in middle school. When I wrote a note telling Matt Turner I had a crush on him and he wrote back telling me I was too tall to be pretty, I'd cried for an hour at Haddie's house, and Natalie had French-braided my hair and told me that high school boys were so much nicer, and then we'd all be in college, so who cared about Matt Turner and his abnormal obsession with college football stats, anyway?

Now she hated me.

"Natalie! Shut up. *Go away.*" Haddie jumped up and slammed the door in her sister's face.

"I'm looking out for you, Haddie!" Natalie yelled. "That's my job! I hope you got an *apology*!"

"It's called *saving my life*," Haddie yelled back.

I heard Natalie stalk back down the hall to her own bedroom, and that was it—I was crying.

"Kate. God. I'm sorry. She's just . . ." Haddie shook her head. "It wasn't like she made it sound."

"It wasn't?" I asked.

"Well . . ." She looked down at her nails. They were painted bright blue. It made me think of Taylor, and the way she always painted her ring finger a different color. "I got . . . sad. Sometimes. It felt like—like you didn't like me anymore? I guess? And I didn't know why. I didn't know what I had *done*. Or if you were mad at me."

"I wasn't mad at you." I tucked my legs in, with my knees up by my chin. "I just made new friends. You can't be the only one I ever talk to."

"I know that," said Haddie, her voice cracking. "But your new friends were so mean to me."

Taylor and Violet and Amira, whispering about Haddie. Making fun of her clothes. Starting a rumor that she'd asked Ernie Vazquez to go out with her even though she hadn't, and that he'd shot her down, even though he was even lower on the popularity scale than she was.

That hat. That ice.

"I know," I said. "I'm sorry."

"You don't have to—"

"Yes, I do," I said, wiping my face clean. "Natalie's right. I should say sorry. I'm sorry that when I started making new friends, I didn't bring you along with me. And I'm sorry that I didn't have your back when they were jerks. I should have. To be honest, it just felt good to hang out with people who hadn't known me my whole life. It's like I could be a different person. And sometimes, being my actual self this year felt crappy. With my mom and stuff. I wanted someone who didn't really care that much, if that makes sense, because then I wouldn't have to . . . talk about things we're talking about right now."

Haddie raised an eyebrow. "But why are you friends with people who don't really care about you?"

"I don't know," I said honestly. "Like, nothing can touch Taylor, and when I'm in her weird little force field, nothing can touch me either. It sounds so *stupid* . . ."

"It *is* stupid," said Haddie.

Something about the way she said it, just flat and serious—it didn't make me mad. It made me laugh.

She laughed too. A little at first, and then we were practically doubled over. It was like that night in Walmart, our stomachs almost hurting. Laughing and laughing, two girls feeling like they could float away. I lay on her scratchy green-and-gold rug, covering my face with my hands. Haddie squeaked, like she always did, which made us laugh harder. We were a tear-streaked, messy-haired pair of complete and utter messes. And there it was again, that feeling I'd had in California:

This is my best friend. *This* is the girl I want to spend weekends with. *This* is where I belong.

"Girls!" Haddie's mom called. "Soup's on, if you're hungry!"

"Come on," said Haddie. "Let's go downstairs and eat. Then we'll go into Natalie's room and change her laptop background to a picture of our eyelids pulled up. She hates when I do that."

WHEN I GOT HOME THAT NIGHT, DAD WAS ON THE PHONE. IT didn't take a genius to see that it was with my mom. He was pacing back and forth with these ridiculous Santa Claus socks on, rubbing his face with his hand, looking like he needed a ten-hour nap.

He hadn't heard me come in, so he just kept right on talking.

"Case, I get that, I do, but you also need to look at some facts. Like that you have a twelve-year-old who is completely devastated right now."

I stood cautiously in the living room. I didn't want to make too much noise.

"Is that what I said? Did I *ever* say that? That's not what I'm *saying*. I'm saying that she has a lot on her plate, with this Haddie thing, and now basketball, and she doesn't need all of this extra . . . stuff." He stood, listening to her talk. "Oh, for the love of—"

Bark, bark, bark! Crap—I'd been spotted. Watson bolted out of the kitchen to see me, excitedly jumping up on the sweats Haddie had lent me, making my dad turn and look.

"Oh—Kate—hey. Casey, she just walked in. Do you want . . . okay. I'll tell her. Yup." He hung up without saying goodbye.

"She didn't even want to talk to me," I said, feeling numb.

Dad looked at me and sighed. "You know what we need?"

"For everyone to stop lying and crying and running away?"

"Yes. And also, pizza."

"Whoever said pineapple doesn't belong on pizza should be thrown in prison," Dad said an hour later. I think the pizza delivery man had been a little surprised to deliver two large pizzas to a guy and his daughter, but there were only a couple of slices left. I considered Juliet's soup an appetizer. I wondered if I should enter one of those eating competitions on TV. Watson begged for a crust and I handed him one, which was probably the happiest moment of his day. If you're feeling that there's too much pizza in this story, well, I can't help you there. McAllisters like cheesy carbohydrates.

"I'm still mad at you," I said. "Although this peace offering was delicious."

"I'm not above food bribes," said Dad. "You stayed with me for a week once when I was in the police academy, and I was trying to study for this big exam. I just kept giving you Cheerios to keep you occupied, and before I knew it, you'd eaten an entire box."

"That's why I'm so tall," I said. "All that nourishment."

"Yes. Cheerios and genetics. Truly the magic combo. I was living in this tiny little bedroom of an apartment. Your mom was between leases. Oh my gosh, keeping you busy that week was impossible."

"So she was pawning me off even then," I said flatly.

Dad looked at me. "It's never been 'pawning you off,' Kate. I'm your *dad*. I *love* taking care of you."

"As much as you love lying?"

"I didn't want to play this card but, shuffle-shuffle-shuffle, you lied to me too. Your mom never told you she had hit Diamond."

"That is *not* as bad as your lie and you know it."

Dad sighed, wiping his hands on a napkin. "We're doing this? You're ready? Okay. I'm *sorry*. And I know your mom is too. We didn't know what to say. Mom went out to Salt Lake City as a last-ditch thing. Her downline was all dropping away; she was hardly making any money. A lipstick here or there—it's not enough to keep the lights on, let alone take care of another human being. The rent was due, and she asked me for help. And I would've given it. I would've. But I had paid the rent on that—well, excuse my language, but—that you-know-what-hole for three months. And your mom just wasn't seeing that this True U thing had to be done with. She had to get a job, or go to school, or something. So I told her no, okay? I told her that maybe you should crash with me for a little bit, till she got firmer on her feet. I'd been telling her that for a while. I didn't realize . . . that she was going to leave the *state*. She thought going to Utah would really fix everything, and that she'd be back soon enough as a Ruby-level seller or whatever."

"Diamond," I said hollowly. A Diamond seller: we had dreamed about that for so long. It had been the center of the vision board that always hung on the wall of wherever we lived. Smiling photos of me and her, pictures of literal money she'd printed out from the internet, cruise ships and beaches and a nice house with a backyard. And in the center of it all: a diamond.

"But it didn't. There are so many sellers out there, and besides, if people want makeup, they go to the mall.

Things were even worse. Everything dried up. True U even got sued, and that sure didn't help things. Your mom wasn't in a good . . . headspace. She's having a really hard time right now. And nobody gets more frustrated with her than me, okay? *Nobody*. But I'm worried about her right now. I called her mom yesterday . . ."

"Grandma?" I asked. Grandma Whalen was . . . well, one of a kind. Haddie's grandma baked cookies and knit blankets for the local pregnancy help center. Grandma Whalen smoked a lot of cigarettes and owned a pit bull. She lived in a trailer outside Chicago.

"I don't know!" Dad threw his hands in the air. "I'm trying to figure it out. I think she maybe needs to talk to someone. A therapist or . . . I don't know. But she came back, because she was out of money, and she asked me not to tell you so that she'd have time to get on her feet. And I didn't want to tell you because I don't want you seeing her right now. She's not being responsible."

"But . . ." I was just so *tired*. I couldn't even cry. So what came out of my mouth was:

"But I *love* her."

And I did. I loved her even though we moved all the time, even though she hounded my friends' moms to ditch their jobs and become #GirlBosses. I loved her even though we had to buy the ice cream that came in a box instead of a carton, if we even got ice cream at the store. I loved her even though she never came to basketball games, and I loved her even though she wasn't there right that second. She was my mom, and I loved her, and I *needed* her.

Dad looked surprised. "Oh, Kate. Of course you do. Of *course*, Bird. Come here." He wrapped me up in a hug and I laid my head on his shoulder. I was so, so tired. I could have fallen asleep right there.

"Let me call her again tomorrow. And then I'll try to get an update, okay? Maybe we could all get together for dinner. That would be great, wouldn't it?"

"Yeah," I said. I loved my dad, too, so much in that moment. And I realized something: my mom, my dad, they weren't just that. It sounds so stupid. To have to *realize* that. But Mom wasn't just Mom. My mom was also Casey Whalen, a person with wants and dreams who has thoughts in her head—thoughts beyond how many points I scored in a basketball game. She had her own complicated history, one that had crashed into my dad's and turned into me. And my dad was *also* Sam McAllister, who had a past and life of his own, who had aced the police academy exam even though he'd had to study with a toddler at his feet.

You want people to be just one thing: the thing that

they are to *you*. But they're not. They're so, so much more. We are complex creatures, every single one of us, and knowing that simple fact is enough to break your heart.

Monday morning during science, Taylor and I had to draw a picture of mitosis happening. The problem was, neither of us had any idea what mitosis was. So we mainly guessed, snuck peeks at Maggie Lawton and Logan Hoyt's paper, and talked.

"Stephanie said she saw some celebrity chef tweet out my video of you and Haddie. I can't believe people are still talking about that," Taylor said.

"That's wild," I agreed. To be honest, so much of the Kate the Great mania had calmed down. And I liked it that way.

"I thought they'd have found something different to geek out about. Anyway. Did you see the new Taylor Swift music video?"

"No. I went to bed kind of early. When did she release it?"

"Midnight. I saw it this morning. It's *so* funny. It has all these zebras. And, like . . . what do you call that animal? The big bird?"

"An ostrich?"

"Ostriches! She has ostriches, and one starts flying, which—"

"Wait, one starts *flying*? Ostriches don't fly," I said.

"Yes, they do!"

"No"—I laughed—"they definitely don't. Google it."

"Um, I'm *going to*. At lunch. Because seriously, I know they do. I've seen one!"

"You have *not*," I said, and we were laughing. Hard. These moments: these were what I didn't want to lose. We laughed about those stupid birds for a full two minutes before Ms. Irvine came over to check on our progress and made us reread the mitosis chapter of our books in silence for ten minutes. Even then, I'd glance up at Taylor, and she'd flap her hands like she was flying, and we'd laugh again.

After science, as we walked to lunch, she threw her arm around me.

"I've missed you lately," she said.

"I see you every day." I laughed.

"I *know*. But I thought maybe you were too celeb now," she joked. "Kate the Great."

"I hate being called that," I said honestly. "I'm glad it's kind of blown over. And I never was too *celeb* for anybody. Ew."

"'Kay. Good. Because you know you're my best friend, right?"

"Duh." I flapped my ostrich wings, which got us laughing again.

We got to the lunchroom and I froze, wondering for just a split second where I should sit. After the time I spent at Haddie's, I felt a sense of . . . belonging, again, with her. I had even told myself this morning as I ate cereal that, okay, I could do this—maybe some days sit with Haddie, some days sit with my other friends. But Taylor yanked me toward our usual table, with Violet, Amira, Brett, and Nico. I was unwrapping my soft pretzel when Haddie walked up, looking like she was on a mission.

"Hi," she said.

A heavy quiet fell over the table as everyone turned to look at her. Haddie, with her hair falling into her eyes, in shoes that had doodles on them.

In her room, laughing about her sister.

"Hi," I said, feeling bold. Violet raised an eyebrow at Taylor, who was watching me.

"I was wondering, if . . . um . . . I could sit here?" She held up her lunch tray and nodded at an empty chair. Then smiled at me.

Haddie! Haddie was doing this for *me*. I had said I wanted her to be friends with Taylor, and here she was, trying. It was one of those small moments of fierce bravery that you feel can move mountains.

"Yes," I said, having a moment of my own. "Of course."

Everyone was silent as Haddie sat down and unwrapped her sandwich. They weren't watching her—they were watching Taylor, who was watching me. I looked down at my food.

"So . . . anyone done with their history project yet?" Haddie asked. "Violet, you have Crispus Attucks, right?"

"Yeah," Violet said flatly. Another moment of silence.

"I have Sybil Ludington," Amira said suddenly. I could have hugged her. *Thank you, thank you, thank you.* "She saved, like, an entire town when she was only sixteen. Isn't that cool?"

Haddie looked so relieved someone had spoken that I felt bad for her.

"That's cool," said Haddie. "I'm doing—"

"Wait, Violet. Are those the jeans from Hollister you were looking at last weekend?" Taylor interrupted her, as if Haddie wasn't even talking.

"Yeah. I had to spend three weeks of babysitting money," said Violet. "But I think my butt looks pretty good."

"Ew," Nico said. Brett chimed in, "If by good, you mean *big.*"

Everyone was laughing, which—it was weird. Talking about someone's butt who was sitting right there. But Violet laughed, too, and it all just felt wrong and

233

awkward and jumbled. I wished I was at our old table with Haddie. And she looked annoyed too.

"Actually, I think I'll just . . . eat in the library or something," said Haddie, standing up. Nobody said goodbye, but Amira gave a little wave.

"Oh, and Kate," said Haddie, "I'm excited for Friday."

"Right," I said, remembering her birthday. I wasn't sure why she was bringing it up right that second, since it was only Monday, but whatever.

Taylor turned to me so quickly her ponytail hit Violet in the face; Violet rubbed her cheek and muttered a quick *ow*. "What do you mean, Friday? You're coming to Ella's Deli. With us. Right?"

Crap. Crap! How could I have been so stupid? Friday, Haddie's birthday. Friday, ice cream date. I'd said yes to both. And now Haddie and Taylor were staring at me, confused, hurt . . . and mad.

"Oh my gosh. I forgot. I forgot both. I . . ."

"But you said you were coming over," said Haddie.

"She has plans," snapped Taylor. "Wake up, Haddie. Your guys' five seconds of fame is over, and Kate doesn't have to pretend to be your friend anymore."

And that was it. You can just snap sometimes, when the moment hits you. You are fine and fine and fine until you're very much Not Fine. When you have *hurt* plus *anger*, it can come out in a fierce moment of fire. My heart just kept on beating, reminding me that I, too, was a person of my own.

I took a deep breath.

One minute of insurmountable courage. I had saved someone's *life*. I could do this.

"Taylor . . . I'm really, really sorry. I told Haddie I'd do this first, and I just forgot. And it's her birthday on Friday, but we could do Ella's Deli next week. Or anytime, really. So I feel like I should go with her. And I'm not *pretending* to be her friend. I *am* her friend."

Taylor stared at me, and in that moment, something was decided. The way I had laid down my cards, she was now laying down hers. The ostrich joke was a distant memory. There would be no more lunch drop-offs from Stephanie for me.

"Fine," she said. That *fine*: it was as dark and stormy as the start of a horror movie. "I'm going to the bathroom." She stood and grabbed her bag, taking off. Violet and Amira jumped up and ran after her, and the boys, who hadn't really been paying attention, were punching each other in the arm for who knows what reason. I could have yelled after Taylor, but I knew there was no point. Something was done. Haddie smiled, and said she was excited, and I tried to be happy. But I knew something. I knew that something was coming, and that Taylor—well, she had a plan. She always did. I just didn't know what it was. But I knew the beginning of a storm when I saw one.

HERE'S THE GOOD THING ABOUT BEING A GREAT TEAM THAT also just happens to be lucky: We didn't feel stressed out that the championship game was on Saturday. We felt excited. Honestly, most of us just couldn't believe we'd made it that far.

Even Coach Watt seemed happy. Maybe it was the fact that it was one of the first truly warm days too. We were in short sleeves, and McDonald's had Shamrock Shakes, and you could wear Sperrys instead of winter boots. It gave everyone this bouncy, breezy feeling. The gym door was pushed open so the sun could hit us and charge our batteries. Plus, the Wisconsin Badgers were going to the Elite Eight. So, that squeak of basketballs on the court? It could almost make me forget that my best friend hated my guts at the moment.

"Saturday night, after-party at my house. Win or lose," said Houa, as we jogged our final lap. "Mom told

Coach we were getting cake from Carl's Cakes."

"Don't torment me," groaned Alex. "Mom has us all on a gluten-free thing."

"Can't wait," I said, tightening my ponytail. Because who was I? I was Kate the Great, and I made my own plans. Taylor Tobitt wasn't my professional scheduler. If I wanted to go to a basketball party, I'd go to a basketball party.

"You're coming?" said Houa. "Awesome!"

"Of course I'm coming," I said.

A few of the girls glanced at each other.

"You're just usually busy," said Dawn bluntly. "With Taylor and them? Don't get mad. It's just the truth."

"I'm not mad," I said, feeling my face get hot. "I want to come."

"Well, of course you should be there. *Duh*. It's a team party," said Houa, knocking her shoulder into mine.

"Girls, listen up," said Coach Watt, gathering us around. "Saturday's game is going to be the toughest we've faced. The Sennett Stars are no joke. Half their team plays for Southeast." That freaked us out. The Southeast Wisconsin Cardinals was the club team you had to try out for. They traveled around during the summer, playing in Indianapolis and Chicago and all kinds of cool places. Even Dawn hadn't made their team. "So this week, we're going to give practice our all. But you know what we have? Hustle. Heart. Teamwork, right?"

"Right," we chanted.

"Knights on three."

"One, two, three, *Knights*!"

"Kate."

I looked up and there was Dad, standing by the doors of the gym in his police blues.

"*Whee-oh, whee-oh,*" sang Maya, mimicking a siren. Alex flicked her in the temple, which I appreciated.

"Hey, Officer. We're all finished up here. Girls, I'll see you tomorrow," Coach Watt said.

I jogged over to Dad. "Hey. I was gonna catch a ride with Houa's mom."

"Car," he said. "Now."

There it was—that look. Not just of seriousness, but of *fear*. My dad was a cop. He charged into buildings with a *gun*. He wasn't afraid of anything in the world. But I'd seen him look scared twice in my entire life. Once when he'd run up to me in the ambulance after I saved Haddie. The other time was when I was in third grade and I watched him on the news, talking to a reporter about a kid at the high school who'd pulled a knife. Scared, *really* scared.

This was serious. This wasn't me being in trouble.

We hurried out to his car. He opened the front door, shoved me in, and— Was that a reporter? The Channel 6 truck, in front of East Middle. Was my video making the rounds again?

"Don't talk. Don't say a word until we're home," he said. "I cannot talk about this until we're home."

"You're scaring me," I said shakily.

Then, he did something even crazier. He turned the *lights* on. He had never, *ever* done that with me—not when I was late to school, not when I had to go to the ER for busting my temple open at the park in second grade—never. We sped home, passing the cars who pulled over for us, whipping into Windy Willow Brook.

We jumped out and went inside, Dad closing the door behind me, locking it.

"Couch," he said. I sat down, and he pulled something up on his iPhone, hooking it up to the TV.

It was a video. *The* video, of me and Haddie? No, not quite. The same level of graininess, the same day, for sure. Same angle. Haddie, looking upset, the pink hat—flying through the air. Tossed from person to person. Violet sneering, Brett shouting, Nico laughing, the person holding the phone—Taylor—silent.

Tossed to me. In a bright purple jacket.

My hands on it—chaos, reaching, throwing—
Onto the pond.

And the rest of the video plays—Haddie going to get it, the ice breaking, me saving her. The same thing we've seen a million times.

I watched that video and I felt that full truth: *That was not on purpose. I did not throw that hat to be mean.* But anyone watching that video would think that's exactly what I had done.

It ended, and the room was silent. I felt like I couldn't breathe. I mean, I really, truly, felt like my heart was pounding too fast.

"This was sent to me this afternoon. At work. Uploaded to YouTube around three o'clock," Dad said. "Channel 6 saw it . . . or were sent it. I'm not sure. But they're playing it tonight."

I blinked.

No.

No.

"Kate," Dad said, "what did you *do*?"

What did I *do*?

Ask me what I *didn't* do.

Ask me how I didn't crumble like a cookie when our lights were shut off, when we moved overnight, when I had to sleep on the couch because we could only afford a one-bedroom. Ask me how I shut down, off, like those same light switches. Ask me how I hurt people. How I watched my best friend be mocked, tormented, by my other best friend. Ask me how I kept my mouth shut, zipped tight, because for once—for *once*—I had some type of power. A power that grew into my heart and took it over, curling around it, crushing it into dust. A power that felt strong. Ask me how Kate the Great, Kate the Kind, Kate the Quiet had turned into Kate the Monster.

But ask me what I didn't do. I didn't throw that hat onto that pond on purpose.

I had wanted it to stop. I had wanted it to be over. That hat had practically burned my hands, and it had been flung, but not completely by me, and not in an effort to ruin anyone's life.

That what-did-you-do question from Dad, it turned into, well, not a *plan*. There wasn't a *plan*. But there was action. There was me, sitting next to Dad as we drove to Taylor's house—that huge, stark-white house. There was Dad, fuming, not speaking to me on the way over, but speaking *loudly* to Taylor's father in the kitchen. There Taylor and I were, in her room. The room I'd *slept* in a million times this year.

"How *could* you?" I sobbed. "You know it wasn't like that video made it look!"

"How could I? How could *you*?" she hissed, venomous. A snake. And in that moment, I saw her as one. "I don't even know who you are. Going on TV. Acting like some kind of *celebrity*, with Haddie Freaking Marks, and then thinking you were just going to ditch me for her? Thinking you could just push me aside like—like *garbage*?"

"Pushing you *aside*? I wasn't pushing you *aside*!"

Taylor shrugged. "Yeah, well, if it makes you feel any better, I'm definitely not aside now! Everyone's going to hate me too. Your name isn't the only one that's out there. They said my name on Channel 6, that very first night. *I'm* the one who sent them the video. So what if Haddie didn't name us? The whole world thinks I'm a bully, too, now."

"So why did you do it?!" I asked desperately. I was out-of-control crying, the kind of crying where you can barely catch your breath. "You've ruined my *life*. The whole world thinks I'm a monster!"

"You did that yourself," snapped Taylor. "You shouldn't have acted like . . ."

"Like *what*?"

"Like you were *better* than me! So *nice*. Nice little

Kate, everyone's friend, basketball star. Well, guess what? You might let Haddie sit at our lunch table. You might have even saved her life. But you're the reason she risked it in the first place. And this whole time, I let you just go on, hanging out with Cory Seymour, living this fantasy of being a hero. I cut the original video to be *nice*. Because I thought we were friends. I didn't know it was going to turn you into this whole other person. Kate the Great? More like Kate the *Liar*. You think you're this good person, deep down, better than the rest of us? Well, guess what, Kate. You and me? We're the *same*."

"No," I choked out. "I would *never* do what you did."

"Ruin someone's goody-goody reputation? If you hadn't known how to save someone from the ice, you would have ruined a lot more than that for Haddie," said Taylor angrily. "So think about *that* next time you try to humiliate me in front of everybody!"

"It was a trip to get *ice cream*!" I sobbed. "God, Taylor, you are such a—"

"I'm a what, Kate?" she asked me, her eyes narrowed. "I'm a lot of things. I am not perfect. But at least I know who I am. I wish I could say the same for *you*."

And just then, I caught a glimpse of the mirror behind her, where she had a thousand photos taped up. There we were, front and center, at the winter dance. I'd felt so happy that night, our cheeks squished together, our eyes sparkling. She'd spent two hours at the mall helping me find the perfect dress, and then stood with me all night even though boys asked her to dance and nobody asked me. I'd seen that photo a thousand times. But right now, I couldn't believe how far away those two girls felt.

"Katherine!" barked Dad. "Get in the car. We're leaving. And *you*," he said to Taylor's dad, "will be hearing from our *lawyer*."

"Taylor," her dad said flatly, "say goodbye to Kate."

I followed Dad downstairs, out the door, and into the car. As soon as I buckled my seat belt, I pulled out my phone.

"Kate, don't look," Dad told me.

But there it was.

Channel 6.

The *Wisconsin State Journal*.

And Cory Seymour. His tweet. *I'm disappointed to learn that Kate McAllister isn't who I thought she was.*

"You should have told me, Kate," said Dad. "We could have figured it out."

"I didn't know," I said. Tears again—how could I possibly have more? "Dad, I swear, I didn't know. It was all so fast. You can see it in the video. I was trying to grab it from Violet. I wanted them to *stop*. And maybe now . . . since everyone knows . . . everything will stop."

"Oh, Bird," he sighed. "Things are just getting started."

21

I LAY IN MY BED THAT NIGHT STARING AT THE CEILING. THIS room, that had seemed so filled with hope, now felt ridiculous. I couldn't even remember the girl who had been so excited about it. All I could think about was Haddie, wherever she was, feeling whatever she was feeling. Through all of this, I hadn't even gotten to talk to her. Dad had taken my phone. He said he didn't want me looking at the internet.

I heard my dad out in the living room, picking up the remote. Cautiously flicking over to the national news. The president had done something stupid that day, apparently, because some old dude with gray hair was going off about him. But he must have switched to local news, because then I heard it—a woman, talking about me. Whether or not I should get *arrested*.

I opened my backpack, but of course I couldn't do any homework either. We hadn't even eaten dinner, but

I wasn't hungry. I went over to the door and pressed my ear against it to hear better.

The worst type of bully.

Why is this okay?

You have to blame the parents. She's a child. Where's her mother?

Ha. Good question.

I heard Dad calling a few people. He really did talk to a lawyer, but it was Nathan, one of our friends from church. Nathan had a daughter my age who went to Sacred Heart School, and we'd known them since I was little. He was one of those people you wanted on your side in an emergency. I heard Dad call the chief and tell him he wouldn't be in tomorrow. He left a voice mail for Mom too.

Finally, after ten, he knocked on my door.

"Kate. Open up. I come bearing food."

I opened the door to Dad holding out a plate with a peanut butter and honey sandwich on it.

"Okay. First, before I say anything, I want you to tell me what happened. Do not leave a thing out, and do not lie to me."

We sat on my bed, and between bites of sandwich, I told him.

I told him *all of it*. Sitting next to Taylor in science,

becoming a member of her crew. Not sitting with Haddie at lunch. Moving up the popularity chain. The way Taylor's group of friends made fun of Haddie, made fun of *lots* of people, and the way I didn't say anything. Basketball being canceled on that warm Wednesday that now felt like a million years ago. Our group of friends hanging out, like we'd hung out a thousand times before, only on this horrible, horrible day, we ran into Haddie. That I honestly, *honestly* didn't mean to throw the hat onto the ice, and that I hadn't even realized I had—that I had meant to try to grab it away from Violet. That it had all happened so fast, and I was scared of how it would look, and I hadn't been sure that I was the reason Haddie was on the ice until I saw the full video. That I was terrified.

When I was done talking, Dad nodded.

"I believe you."

"You should! I'm telling the truth!"

"Listen, Bird. I know you. I've known you since before you were *you*. Those people on the news—on the internet? They don't. People *love* tearing other people's lives apart. Nathan said that the best course of action is to stay completely silent."

"But they're saying stuff that isn't true!"

"Kate! This isn't about proving to the world you're

a nice person. It's about trying to keep your name out of the news. Nathan knows what he's talking about, and I think we should listen. No interviews, no nothing. You're not going to school for the rest of the week."

"But if I don't go to school, I can't go to basketball."

"Yeah, *no*. You're not going to a public basketball game, Kate. We're on lockdown. I'll call Coach tomorrow."

The party at Houa's. My chance to finally feel like a real part of the team.

"But Dad—"

"Kate, I am the dad, and you are the kid. And I know you may not be used to operating that way, but I'm pulling rank at the moment. You are not getting your phone back until this dies out. I will call the school and get your homework assignments for you. You are never—*ever*—to speak to Taylor again. And tomorrow morning, you may make exactly two phone calls."

"To who?"

"To your mom, because I think you need her right now. And to Haddie, to apologize."

Haddie. She had to have seen the video by now. Her birthday—the whole reason this had happened in the first place. No way was I going now. It was all for nothing.

"We are not answering the door. We are not answering emails. We are hoping someone else does something more stupid tomorrow, and we are not going to let this ruin us. Right?"

"Right," I mumbled.

"Now go to sleep. It's late."

Of course, I couldn't sleep.

I had dreams of Cory Seymour and Kendra, showing up at my door, shoving a camera in my face. She was wearing all True U makeup.

When I woke up in the morning, I came out into the living room to find Dad watching the news. He quickly turned it off, but not before I heard someone on TV tell Maria Ramirez that I was the reason kids had depression.

"I did something bizarre," Dad said.

"Um, okay?"

"I went to Walmart at six a.m. You know who goes to Walmart at six a.m.? Truck drivers. It was me and a bunch of guys who looked like they should be named Butch or Rex or something. But I bought this," he said. He pushed a box toward me. "A five-thousand-piece puzzle. I thought we'd need something to do that didn't involve live TV or internet."

"You thought right."

"I called your mom this morning, and I also talked to Haddie's mom."

"You stole my phone calls. What *time* is it?"

"It's almost ten. Mom didn't answer, but Haddie's mom is . . . upset. So is Haddie. She stayed home from school today and is awaiting your call. Juliet and I thought it would be best if you two talked directly. I disabled the internet on your phone, so don't even think about it," he said, holding out my iPhone.

"You're really not going in to work?"

"I told you, I have days saved up. Besides, the squad . . . they're family. They get it. They've got our backs."

I kept thinking of people I loved seeing that video and hating me. Mrs. Urbanski, Houa's mom, even Mrs. Levine. They'd all see it and think I was a bully. Think I was *Taylor*.

I went into my room and closed the door before dialing Haddie. She picked up immediately.

"I can't believe you," she said. Her voice sounded hoarse, like she'd been crying all night.

"Haddie . . ."

"How could you—how could you *do* that to me? How could you lie to my *face*?"

"Haddie, I didn't know. I *swear* I didn't know. I was trying to make them *stop*. I meant—to fling it away, not throw it onto the ice."

"You didn't *know*? Who doesn't know what their own *hands* are doing?"

"Someone stupid," I said desperately. "Me. I was so, so stupid. I—"

"And you took me to California, and acted like . . . things were going to be different. But they weren't. Did you—were you all just *laughing* at me this whole time?"

"Haddie, *no*." My voice was shaking. "It wasn't . . . it wasn't like that. It was an accident. I didn't know. I brought you to California because I wanted to. I missed you. I promised I'd go to the birthday dinner because I want to be friends again. I'm sorry, I *told* you, I'm sorry for—"

"Natalie was right," said Haddie hollowly. "She said I shouldn't trust you anymore, and she was right. You and me? We're *done*."

"Please don't do this," I choked out.

Silence. I pulled the phone away from my cheek—the call had ended.

I let out a sob, and Dad came in. He opened his arms and I fell into them, crying hard.

"We will get through this. And we will come out

the other end with some big lessons learned. I know it doesn't feel like that right now," he said.

"It feels like the entire world hates me and I have no friends," I mumbled into his shoulder.

"*I* don't hate you. Mom doesn't hate you. And soon, this will blow over. Just like Kate the Great went away, so will Kate the Bully."

"Is that what they're calling me?"

"Never you mind that. Come on. Let's do that stupid puzzle and watch some mind-numbing Netflix."

We went back into the living room. Dad heated up some water for tea and called in some Chinese take-out, even though it was ten a.m. Crab rangoon can heal a lot of emotions. I lay down on the couch and flipped Netflix to *The Great British Baking Show*. I just wanted to watch polite British people bake scones and forget that my life was a dumpster fire.

The entire day, we lived in a cave. Dad would check the news occasionally on his phone and get mad, *really* mad, then call Nathan and be reassured that staying silent was the best course of action. We kept trying to call Mom, but she kept not answering. Dad said a million times that he was happy we rented, because it made it way harder for people to find out where we lived. For the first time, I was grateful for his paranoia.

Midafternoon, a couple of cops stopped by and talked to Dad quietly in the kitchen for a bit. Then I noticed another police car stayed parked in our parking lot, but Dad wouldn't tell me why.

That night, I hugged Dad before I went to bed. I fell into his arms and he squeezed me tight, so tight I could hardly breathe, and for the first time, I felt it: my heart, beating along, the *thump-thump* reminder that I could wake up and take steps and move forward, maybe, just maybe.

THURSDAY MARKED THE THIRD DAY WE STAYED INSIDE. A sudden cold front had moved in, bringing one of those mid-March snowstorms with it. It looked like a winter wonderland outside. Dad was switching shifts and using up vacation time left and right, but he wanted to stay with me until things died down.

They were dying down, at least to the rest of the world. I wasn't a trending topic on Twitter, and no huge news stations had really picked anything up. Dad had even made me cancel my Instagram account.

"I have a question. And it might sound nuts," I told Dad one afternoon as we watched a nerdy guy named Rahul be crowned the Star Baker of the week.

"Hit me," he said.

"Do you think this was bad karma because we took Creepy Jesus down from the wall?"

He cracked up. It was the first time I'd heard him

laugh since The Video.

"I don't think we believe in karma," he said. "You'd have to ask Father Andrew."

"I think I do," I said. "I put bad things out into the world, and now they're coming back to make me miserable. Mom too. All those times she convinced people to spend a hundred bucks for a True U starter kit . . . look how that all turned out for her."

"*Taylor* released that video, Kate, not God. Sometimes His plan—"

"Yeah, yeah, yeah. His plan. It sure seems to suck sometimes. Especially the part where the whole world hates me."

"The world hates a lot of people, but never for long. Besides, if it makes you feel any better, I think most of them hate *me*," Dad said. "They just don't know my name."

I shrugged.

"Okay, here's something I don't get," he said.

"The difference between a Victoria sponge and a génoise?" I said. "Me neither."

"Not the show," he said with an eye roll. "Why . . . why would Taylor release the rest of that video when it makes her and her own friends look horrible?"

It was a fair question. It wasn't just me in that video.

You could see Nico's springy curls, and Violet's face, clear as day.

"Because she doesn't care," I said. "Because Taylor calls the shots. She always has. What are they going to do? Get mad at her? Oust her from her own lunch table? Taylor does whatever she wants. She knows who she is and what she's doing. The news isn't going to publish her or anybody else's name. She's not the one everyone was talking about. People don't care who filmed the video; they care who threw the stupid hat. The worst that will happen is they'll be, like, grounded."

"You know what's funny," Dad said, "is that she sounds kind of like Haddie."

"Haddie and Taylor couldn't be more different."

"In some ways, yeah. But in other ways . . . They're girls who make their own decisions. That's probably part of why Taylor doesn't like her, don't you think?"

"Of course," I said. "You can't be Taylor's friend if you know who you are."

And there it was: an avalanche of truth, crashing down a mountain and trying to bury me alive. *You can't be Taylor's friend if you know who you are.* Well, joke was on me.

Dad stood up. "Self-discovery requires sugar. We need ice cream, yes?"

"Ella's Deli? I'll take a Moose Tracks."

He grabbed his wallet. "You okay here? *Don't* answer the door if anyone buzzes, okay?"

"Won't."

As Dad left, I turned the TV up. The contestants were being asked to make biscuits—not like the kind you get for breakfast, but apparently just British cookies. One of the contestants was so nervous he was practically crying. *Dude, it's a cookie*, I wanted to tell him.

And then I felt bad.

We're all afraid of stupid things. He was afraid of making a chocolate cream biscuit on a Netflix show. I was afraid of Taylor.

Because that's what it was, really. Wasn't it? I was scared. Fear can do strange things to a person; it can take away their voice and hide it in a box. It can give them a mask that's impossible to remove. Fear can turn greatness into a monster.

Brave girl, Kate the Great, going out on a frozen lake. Hauling her friend to safety. Afraid of a seventh-grade girl with icy-blond hair and a cell phone video.

Was I brave or chicken?

Was I great or a bully?

I imagined taking the burden of Taylor and just . . . pulling it off. Like a pair of sweaty gym socks after a game. Peeling away the heavy muck and letting myself breathe. It felt so amazing, I almost started crying, imagining a life where what Taylor thought of what I did or said . . .

Didn't matter.

Where I could decide whose birthday I wanted to go to, or who I wanted to invite to California, or whose lunch table I wanted to sit at—and the choice was mine. Mine alone. Because I wasn't Taylor's best friend or Haddie's old buddy or Casey's daughter or Coach Watt's player. I was Kate McAllister, my very own person, with my very own thoughts. I couldn't make a biscuit on any baking show, but I was a person who could say what she thought.

I knew I probably shouldn't talk to Haddie or Taylor or anybody else if Dad wasn't home. And he had disabled internet access on my phone.

But I knew where I could start.

I went into my room and called Mom. There was no answer. She hadn't updated her Instagram page since the photo of her at the terrace. Her stories had all been ads for True U products, asking people to buy just one more eyeshadow palette so she could qualify for Sapphire level again because *Success is NOT a straight line!!!* 🖤

"Hey, it's Casey Whalen. If you're interested in purchasing a True U product, please hit up my website at TrueU dot com slash CaseyWhalenBeauty. Otherwise, leave a message!"

"Mom?" I said. "It's me."

I sat in silence for a second, which felt weird on a voice mail. What could I say to her?

Kate the Great would say that she missed her mom, and that she was proud of her for following her dreams, and that she understood the lie.

Kate the Bully would say that she hated her mom, that she was a liar, that Kate was better off with her dad, and that she never wanted to see her again.

And me? What would *I* say?

"I miss you," I said, my voice breaking. "And I'm mad at you, Mom. I'm really, really mad at you. I don't know why you won't talk to me. I don't get why you're staying away. But I'm tired of feeling like I'm not special enough to make you care about me more than a bunch of makeup." A tear slipped out. Two. I felt like a mirror that had a little crack in it, and someone touched it in the wrong place and it shattered. "I wish that having me was enough, and that I didn't feel like you were always trying to chase something better. But I . . ." I coughed a little. "I was thinking about that time in Moose Junction. With the stars. And I missed you, and I wanted to call and say that I love you. I still do. A lot. Okay? Bye."

I hung up the phone and dissolved into a thousand pieces. Dad was suddenly there, arms around me. He'd heard the whole thing, walking in when I hadn't noticed.

"You did real good, Kate," he murmured into my hair. "You spoke the truth."

"She's going to be so upset."

"You can't control that. You can't make people feel any emotion you want them to. People can't be *forced* into understanding. All you can control is yourself."

"And what about everyone else? Am I supposed to leave Taylor a voice mail telling her what a terrible person she is?"

Dad cocked an eyebrow. "Hmm."

"What?"

"It's just—you spent a lot of time with her. Is she really a terrible person?"

"She ruined my entire life!"

"First of all, there's no evidence of a *ruined life* here, okay? Secondly . . . Kate. I just—I was driving. And thinking about how mad I was at her. And then I remembered that Juliet probably wanted to murder me before we talked."

"So?"

262

"*So*, people get mad. I'm mad at Taylor. I'm *furious* at that girl. Haddie's mom was furious at me, and you; probably still is, a little. But we're just trying our best. And, I don't know . . . maybe Taylor is, too, in a way. She's a kid. You're a kid. Haddie's a kid."

"So what? Kids can do big, evil things."

"Well, sure. *Sure.* But kids can also hurt. And hurt people hurt people. I think Taylor is a very hurt person."

I'd never thought of Taylor as a hurt person. I thought of Taylor as a *powerful* person, but maybe Dad and I were both right—flip sides of the same coin. Power can be used for good, or power can be used to release an incriminating video clip or tease someone about their hair. *Power* can make sure everyone knows that you cannot be messed with, cannot be abandoned, cannot be left.

Only a hurt person would do that. Only a *left* person would make sure people could not leave, and punish them if they did.

"The thing about Taylor is . . . everyone at school is kind of afraid of her, but it's like she's everyone's ruler, at the same time. Except the basketball girls. They couldn't care less. I wish I could play on Saturday."

"Sorry, Bird. The East Knights will have to live without their rebound queen."

"They'll manage. But . . ." I chewed my lip. "I guess I felt like the girls on the team were starting to actually become my *real* friends. And this messes that up. A lot."

"Well," said Dad, "real friends know who we are, and care about us despite our faults."

"When did you become an expert in twelve-year-old girls?" I asked.

"Night classes. Dad School. How am I doing? Getting an A?"

"I'd say a solid B-plus. But you know what?" I said, my brain starting to whir, coughing up dust and stretching its limbs. "I think you just gave me an idea."

FRIDAY MORNING, I WOKE UP EARLY.

"So," said Dad, "you're sure about this?"

"Positive."

I took a hot shower, as hot as I could make it. I wanted to burn the last few weeks off me. I got dressed, pulling on my favorite soft gray T-shirt and a pair of jeans. I threw on a pink infinity scarf Mom gave me for my birthday last year, because say what you will about Mom, but she knew how to fake confidence. And I needed that boost today.

I had convinced Dad to let me go back to school. He'd insisted, somewhat dramatically, in my opinion, on walking me in and speaking to Principal Howe. He agreed to give me my phone back, but without internet. He did give me the gist of what the outside world was saying, though, so I wasn't completely in the dark.

"It's not great, Kate. Everyone in town seems to be

talking about it. Random parents from school complaining to Principal Howe. Even though it's mostly calmed down online, you're not going to be as lucky in the East Middle hallways. And if you're halfway through math class and start to panic, or if you ever feel unsafe in any way, you call me."

I'd promised him I would. Then I had stayed up until midnight, writing. Dad helped, but they were my words. I sent Mr. Collins an email, and I had a response in the morning: *Absolutely. Come to my classroom in the morning.*

When we got to East Middle, there it was: that stupid Channel 6 truck. The reporter was trying to get kids to talk, but he wasn't supposed to share kids' faces without permission from their parents, and parents mostly just drop kids off and drive away. We drove around to the side door, where you could go into the gym. Principal Howe and Coach Watt were right inside, waiting for us. Luckily, all the dumb news people apparently thought I was going to waltz in the front door.

When we got there, I was surprised—Principal Howe actually hugged me. I thought everyone would hate me.

"Oh, Kate. You poor thing. You must be terrified," she said.

"I actually feel okay today," I said.

"Your dad told me you won't be joining us tomorrow, which is . . . unfortunate," Coach Watt said. Principal Howe shot her a look. "But I get it! I do. We'll miss you."

"Kate has a meeting with Mr. Collins," Dad said to Principal Howe. "So I'm going to walk her to his classroom. Then we'll chat in yours, Lila?" She agreed, and he escorted me down the hallway.

If I'd thought everyone was looking at me before, it was nothing compared to now. Literally every person in the hallway was whispering, staring, turning their heads as I went by. I saw Taylor with Violet and Amira by her locker, and I walked right past, not even blinking. They just stared, wordlessly. Everyone seemed completely shocked I was there. I felt completely shocked myself.

Mr. Collins was waiting for me at his desk. He had what I'd emailed him pulled up on his computer screen.

"Can I tell you something, Kate?" Mr. Collins asked.

"Yeah?"

"When all this went down, I know everyone was all rah-rah. Putting you up on a pedestal. And when the rest of that video came out, I was worried about you. I called your dad to make sure you were okay. But I knew you were always the same Kate you'd been. Whether the whole world was cheering you on or the whole world was spitting in your face. But this"—he pointed to the computer, tapping his finger on the screen—"*this* . . . is pretty great."

Five minutes before first bell, Mr. Collins hit Publish. The *Knightly News* had a new blog entry. He also sent it out to the local news and posted it on the East Middle Facebook page, which had been flooded with comments saying the other kids and I should be expelled.

I couldn't resist hiding in a bathroom stall, pulling out my phone to open my Notes app, and reading the words again, for myself.

To whoever is reading this,
    I feel like the entire world has been talking about me for the past few weeks. I was sitting back and letting them, and sometimes joining the conversation, whether it was talking to *The Morning Buzz* or Cory Seymour. But I never really felt like I was saying what I meant. Instead of the world talking about me, I think I need to speak

for myself for a second.

I'm only twelve years old, but I already feel like I've made lots of mistakes in my life. I messed up tying my shoes a lot in kindergarten. When I was eight, I knocked over our Christmas tree and broke my mom's favorite ornament. And in seventh grade, I started spending time with people who didn't like me for who I was.

I wasn't bullying other kids. But I was doing something even worse. I was standing there and not saying anything. I could have been the person who helped other people when they needed it, and instead, I was the chicken.

Then, in an instant, I wasn't. Back in late February, a video clip went viral of me pulling Haddie Marks out of Woodglen Pond. Suddenly, I wasn't a speck of dust. I was Kate the Great. I had always been kind of in the background of everything, but I was all of a sudden front and center. It mostly felt strange, to be on TV and to have people talking about me. But what felt really, truly weird was that I became some kind of superhero in people's minds. I was the ultimate antibully, the one in the cape with the lightning vision or whatever.

The truth is, Haddie was on the pond because she was trying to get her winter hat back. The hat was on the pond because I had tossed it there when attempting to stay out of the game the other kids were playing with it. It was never my intention to toss the hat onto the ice and cause Haddie to try to get it back.

But I don't say any of this to push blame. Because the blame is mine. It doesn't matter if I threw the hat on purpose or not. What matters is that I should have stopped it and stood up for Haddie. Not just that day, but a million other times this year. I can't control what the other kids were doing, but I should have controlled myself. I'm really, really sorry, not just to Haddie, but to every other kid at this school—and all schools—who gets picked on. We may not all be the main mean person. But plenty of us are the people who could step up and make it stop.

I guess I was so used to seeing a bully as a single person. But aren't we all bullies some-times? Don't we all have moments where we do the wrong thing, make the wrong choice, stand with the wrong person? We all have it in us to be the hero, or to be the bully, and we're all making choices every single day that shape who we are. We are so, so much more than one thing, or one incident, or one cell phone video.

I am not Kate the Great, the superhero who saved her best friend and defended her against bullies. I'm also not Kate the Monster, the bully who tried to get a girl killed. I'm just Kate. I hope that, for now, that can be enough.

Signed,

Kate McAllister

7th Grade

East Middle School

I sat in that cold bathroom stall, looking at initials someone had carved into the wall. And then, I copied and pasted the words of the letter into a text message. Found Haddie Marks. Hit Send.

I know things will never be how they were. But I mean every word of this. 🖤 And happy birthday.

The bell rang, and the day began, and I faced the music, as loud and crashing as it seemed.

Mrs. Urbanski came up to me during homeroom and patted me on the shoulder. "That was a wonderful letter, Kate. I'm proud of you," she whispered. I noticed

Haddie still wasn't at school.

The rest of the day dragged on. During science, Ms. Irvine announced that we were switching lab partners for the rest of the semester. I didn't know if it was my dad's doing or Taylor's, but I had a feeling someone had called and requested it. Now I was with Jason Fritz, this kid who always stopped to look at his own reflection when he passed the freshly scrubbed trophy case. Well, he was better than Taylor.

A lot of people were still upset with me. I could tell that much. Logan Hoyt wouldn't scoot her chair in when I tried to get past her to sharpen my pencil. Carmen Cortez, who I was usually kind of friendly with, didn't say a word to me when we washed our hands next to each other in the bathroom.

Walking into the cafeteria, I was terrified. My plan, which Dad and I had come up with together, was to quickly buy a drink and make my way to the library with my sack lunch. I felt like a loser, but nobody was going to dump milk on me in there, at least. If you so much as talked above a whisper, Mr. Kim would threaten you with a week's detention.

I grabbed a soft pretzel and a juice. I glanced out over the lunchroom and saw my usual table, laughing and trying to pretend they weren't looking at me. Where

Haddie usually sat was empty.

I was halfway out of the cafeteria when I felt someone grab my arm. I jumped about a foot in the air and yanked it back.

"Kate! I'm sorry. It's just me." It was Alex. She tucked her hair behind her ears. "Where are you going?"

"Um. I was going to go eat in the library," I admitted. "Kind of . . . get some time to myself."

"Oh. Okay. Well . . . if you need someone to sit with, you can sit with us, okay?"

I stared at her.

"What?" she asked.

"Alex . . ." I looked around. "You don't have to do that."

"Do what? Treat you like a member of the team? Try to be your friend?" She raised an eyebrow. "Kate. We've *been* doing that."

When I was with the girls on the team, I had to admit, I felt more in control. Like I could just be—not Kate the Great, not Kate the Monster.

Kate.

"We won't let anyone say anything to you, okay? Anyone who knows you and saw that video knows you didn't mean to throw that hat on the ice. Dawn said if anyone says anything mean, she'll throw a basketball at their head."

"Principal Howe would say violence isn't the answer," I said with a grin.

"Yeah, well, as long as nobody records it with a cell phone, I think we're good." She linked her arm with mine. "Come on."

I felt confident after lunch. Alex, Houa, Dawn, Maya— they were more than teammates. They were friends, even though I had put them in a Basketball Box. Maybe I really was part of the team, after all.

I called Dad quickly after we ate, hiding in yet another bathroom stall. That place was becoming my office. But I had to know how people were reacting to my letter.

"It definitely caught wind in the news," Dad said. "Maria Ramirez was talking about you again."

"She needs a hobby," I said.

"Agreed. She was nice, though. She talked about how we put too much pressure on our children for perfection, and how quick we are to beat them down. That gray-haired guy on Channel 6 who's been on forever, though—he had your back too. Went off on some random caller trying to call you a monster."

I closed my eyes. "So, most people like me? Or hate me?"

"Fifty-fifty? It's hard to tell. You want to know what *I* think about your letter?"

My heart sped up. "Yeah."

"It made me cry." He cleared his throat. "I'm proud of you every day, Bird. But especially today."

I hung up with Dad and just sat in the stall for a minute, pulling myself together. I could do this. The day was half over. People were *listening*.

Right as I was about to unlatch the lock and walk out of the stall, someone else walked in. I took a deep breath and stepped out of the stall to see—

Taylor.

She was putting lip gloss on in the mirror. We both froze.

Silence.

Taylor focused back on her own reflection and smacked her lips. "This is from Kiki Jakob's new makeup line. Real makeup. Not like the crap your mom sells."

I stood there, blinking.

"You may have written that letter, but you *are* a bully," said Taylor.

I looked at her, *really* looked at her. Her bright pink Kate Spade backpack, her immaculate white jeans. She didn't have a hair out of place. It was like she'd stepped out of an Instagram picture.

But her voice was shaking as she tried to insult me. Her eyes looked scared.

I wanted her to be Taylor the Mean Girl, because that was so *easy*, wasn't it? To think she wasn't a person, just a mean-spirited jerk who wreaked havoc at school?

But the winter dance. When she gave me a photo of us she had framed for Christmas, and also a handwritten letter about how glad she was that we had become friends. When I'd been home sick with strep throat and she had not only brought me all my homework but a big batch of cookies too. Taylor had her own complicated history and a tricky, crooked heart—one that loved hard and hurt hard.

Hurt people hurt people, Dad had said. Well, sure. But loved people loved people. And I was a loved person.

Taylor was right. We *weren't* so different. Not good, not bad, just us. There we stood: Two Girls Without Mothers. Two Girls Who Mess Up.

"I'm sorry," I said, not even sure what for.

She looked surprised.

"I wish . . . things were different," I told her honestly.

Feelings crashing into feelings, sadness crashing

into sadness. The soft *click* of a friendship ending.

"Me too," she said.

The bell rang, and the spell was broken. She turned and left.

WHEN THE FINAL BELL RANG, PRINCIPAL HOWE ESCORTED ME out the side door and into my dad's waiting cop car. That thing used to embarrass the crap out of me. Now I was just grateful. Nobody was going to mess with us in a cop car.

We snuck out the side exit and sped down the street, glancing back at the reporters who were filming B-roll of East Middle and hoping I'd suddenly walk outside.

"You made it," Dad said.

"I did," I acknowledged.

"I'm proud of you, Bird."

"Proud enough to let me play basketball tomorrow?"

"I said proud, not easily convinced."

When we got home, I took out my phone and saw that I had a text from Mom.

I had forwarded her the letter I wrote for the *Knightly News*. And of course, I'd left her the voice mail the night before. I sat on my bed and opened my texts with shaky hands.

Katie lady—you are the greatest gift I've ever been given. I'm sorry for the ways I haven't been a perfect mom. But I will always ♥ you to the ★ ★ ★ and back.

I stared at it, and there was a knock on my door. Dad poked his head in.

"What's up, Bird? You good in here? Not on the internet, are you?"

I held up my phone, and he read the text. He sighed.

"She's not lying, you know. She *does* love you to the stars and back. We both do." He sat on the bed next to me. "This . . . this whole family situation. It sucks for you sometimes. Doesn't it?"

Kate the Great leaped up to say *No, no, no, it's fine, everything's fine.* Monster Kate ranted and raved. I took a deep breath and just let myself feel for a second: not caring about how anyone else would react, not caring about Maria Ramirez or Haddie Marks or Taylor Tobitt. Sitting in my own hurt feelings.

It *did* suck. It sucked that in the twelve years before I moved here I had to keep track of where my toothbrush and socks were at two different houses. That I had to remember Dad kept the spoons to the left of the oven and Mom kept them wherever we had room in our apartment of the moment. It sucked that each parent had a different set of rules, and that I'd have to explain to my friends that yes, I was allowed to stay out until nine the weekend before because I had been at Mom's, but this weekend I was at Dad's, so I had to be home by seven thirty sharp. It sucked that other people got to have smiley pictures taken with their parents at elementary school graduation, when all I got was a selfie with Mom and an awkward photo with Dad, and didn't look very happy in either. It sucked that Dad would say something biting about Mom, and then she would say something sarcastic about Dad, and I was just a sounding board, the go-between, the person who had to keep their mouth shut. It sucked that we'd never be one of those families in the Christmas-morning TV commercials, wearing matching PJs and eating pancakes while we opened presents, all three of us, *together*. It sucked that one of them was always spending important holidays alone, and that one always missed out on having a birthday dinner with me. It sucked that I would always kind of feel like if I hadn't been born, maybe my parents' lives would be better.

And yet.

I had a dad who came to almost every basketball game and rearranged his entire life so that a twelve-year-old girl could move in with him. A dad who would get rid of his office and change his work hours and learn to cook. A mom who had big dreams and saw beyond the everyday here-and-now. A mom who would take me on spontaneous trips with her, promising me that I, too, had a spotlight.

"Sometimes," I said. "But not right this second."

Dad gave me a hug. "We'll see her soon. We just need to give her some time."

"Yeah, I know."

"Hey. Special treat. Cory Seymour . . ."

"You watch vloggers now?"

"I had to see what he said! New video up. Come see."

"Is it going to make me cry?"

"Maybe in a good way."

We went out into the living room and Dad hit play. Cory Seymour was about to interview some country singer, but first, he gave his opening monologue. After going on for a minute about a weird dream he'd had, he dove into a new topic. Me.

"As most of you know, I was so excited to have Kate McAllister on my show last week. I thought, finally— here's a kid who isn't afraid to stand up to bullies and love her friends and do the right thing. For the two of you watching who *haven't* seen the video, Kate was caught on camera saving her best friend's life. The media dubbed her Kate the Great, and we all just went ga-ga over this incredible kid. Of course, earlier this week, a new video emerged showing that just before the rescue took place, Kate had been bullying the very girl she helped to save. And so we pounced on her again. But this time, it was to paint her as the villain in the story. The bully, the liar, the example of everything wrong with America today."

"Um, didn't you say this was supposed to make me feel better?" I asked. Watson jumped into my lap and snuggled in.

"Keep watching."

"And then this morning, Kate posted a public letter on her school's blog. And this letter, it's just fantastic. I'll share the full thing below. But here's what you need to know. It's an apology, but it's also sort of a declaration, reminding us all that . . . Kate's a kid. And it's hard to be a kid. She's doing the best she can. You know, a kid who learns from her mistakes and continues to grow, and isn't afraid to say sorry—that's the kind of kid we want to hold up in our society. And so, listen: I think that Kate McAllister is still Kate the Great."

Dad turned to me, grinning. "I have to admit—I wish you weren't in the news anymore—but Cory Seymour got it. He understood what you were trying to say. And if he did, other people will too."

I wished I felt happy. But really, what I felt was . . . *seen*. In the kind of way that's slightly uncomfortable.

But I really wished they'd cool it with the Kate the Great nickname. I didn't want everyone to love me. I wanted everyone to *understand* me. But more than that, I wanted everything to go back to normal.

"No interviews this time," I said.

"Oh, believe you me. I agree completely," said Dad. "Come on. I'll make you a sandwich."

I was sure Haddie must have read my letter, but I was still surprised when I woke up the next morning to a text from her.

Thanks. One word.

Well. It's not like I deserved any more than that. I knew that things could never go back to how they were, her and me making bracelets by candlelight and swearing to be best friends forever. I was the reason we weren't.

But who knows? Natalie had told us a thousand times how different high school was from middle school. We'd be there in a little over a year. And anything could happen. Isn't that what Haddie had said, a million years ago as we caught those fireflies?

Anything can happen.

Houa had texted, too, asking if I was going to be at the game. I told her no. Dad was supposed to work that morning, but he had traded shifts yet again; he was still a little nervous about leaving me home alone for a long period of time.

It was Saturday morning, and Nathan had stopped by with a huge loaf of spicy cheese bread from the farmers' market and some coffee for Dad. He wanted to see how we were and talk to Dad about some boring legal stuff. Dad really, really wanted to sue Taylor's parents, but I told him that was stupid, and besides, they hadn't done anything. Taylor had. And Nathan advised him that if he wanted to get back into the press for negative media attention, attempting to sue a twelve-year-old was the quickest way to do so.

But that was his issue, not mine. The sun was out, and I had spicy cheese bread. I leaned out onto our balcony and closed my eyes, feeling a slight breeze. You could almost taste summer. Soon it would be here, and so different from all the summers before. It wasn't going to be Mom and me, heading to the beach in Moose Junction and splitting a huge bag of chips, me reading a library book while she drew up a new vision board. It wouldn't be Haddie and me, either, dangling our feet into the pool and talking about how next year everything would be different. The thought that I had probably gone to the pool with Haddie for the last time could have made me sad. But instead, I tried to think of the possibilities. Dad and I had always talked about going to Wisconsin Dells together to spend the weekend hopping around water parks. Maybe we would this summer. Maybe I could invite Alex or Houa. Maybe we could have a team sleepover, all squeezed into Dad's apartment.

"Hey, Kate?" Dad said, sticking his head out. "Nathan just showed me one more clip you might want to see."

I was still on a total internet ban because, according to Dad, people in the world were messed up, and even Nobel Peace Prize winners had their haters. Except for that Cory Seymour clip, I'd been in a digital hole.

Nathan pulled up something from YouTube. It was Maria Ramirez—man, she just couldn't leave me alone. But she was talking to someone else. Haddie.

We huddled around the phone and watched as Maria asked her what had happened.

"I still don't know what to make about . . . what happened that day on the pond. I don't know how I feel, and I don't know why things had to go down the way they did. I probably never will," said Haddie. "But

I *do* know that her letter meant a lot to me. To get an apology was all I really wanted."

"Do you think you'll ever be able to forgive Kate McAllister?" Maria asked her. She might as well have been asking the president about foreign policy, not a seventh grader who her best friend was.

Pause.

Long pause.

"Yeah," said Haddie finally. "I don't think things will ever go back to how they were. But, yeah. I forgive her."

That gift—that heavy load, being pushed off my shoulders. Someone telling me to put it down. I felt so light, I could jump off the balcony and fly to the moon. I felt like I could do anything, anything in the world, the weight of guilt just gone, gone, gone with an uttering of forgiveness from the only person who could truly *give* it.

The clip ended. Dad and Nathan looked at me.

"I think I have somewhere to be," I said.

"Are you asking me or telling me?" said Dad.

"Consider it a beg."

Dad sighed. "Hurry up. We're going to be late."

It's funny—I'd say it usually takes me about thirty minutes to get ready for a basketball game. But that day, I did it in four. I grabbed my jersey, yanked my shoes out of the closet, and begged Dad to turn the sirens on. He wouldn't. But he did drive pretty fast.

As we drove, my phone beeped. I opened it to see a text from none other than Haddie Marks.

Ur big game today? Good luck. 🏀

Kate and Haddie, Haddie and Kate. A story of small moments and big courage—a friendship that had changed and would stay changed forever. But see? Forever changes and happy endings: these things can both be true.

When we got there, Dad hustled me into the Kohl Center, the giant basketball complex on UW's campus where the championship game would take place. Dad, Mr. Rule-Following-Officer McAllister, *did* flash his police badge to let us skip security. I heard a girl yell, "Oh my God, that's Kate the Great!" but we hurried past her. There was more of a crowd than you'd expect for a middle school girls' basketball tournament. The court smelled like nacho cheese and rubber basketballs.

My favorite smells.

I pulled out my maroon ribbon and tried to tie it as we ran. I'd see later in pictures that it was a sloppy mess, with half of my ponytail falling out. But just then, as the East Middle Knights hustled out of their warm-ups to do the pregame huddle, I burst into the gym.

Now that I think about it, there's no way the entire gym fell into a dramatic hush and stared at me. But that's how it felt. It was probably just our team.

I ran over.

"I'm here," I said. "If I can play."

Coach looked at me, looked at the referee, looked at the score clock. She shrugged.

"Sometimes," she said, "it's better to ask forgiveness than permission. Nobody tell your parents I said that. Starters: Houa, Shayla, Dawn, Alex, Kate. But tip the ball and know you're about to be benched for a quarter or two, because you *did* miss practice all week."

I jogged out to the middle of the court, my shoes squeaking. I hadn't warmed up at all and my muscles felt tight. The other girl was taller than me, in a shiny purple jersey. She smiled. She was happy to be there, and so was I. The ref blew his whistle, looked at both of us, and threw the ball in the air. I leaped, high as I could, and grabbed it myself, bringing it down firmly.

My heart was pounding with the *ba-bump, ba-bump, ba-bump* of a score clock and adrenaline and a lesson learned—that you had to take all the things people were to you, the good and bad and jumbled in between. And then, you would go from there: moving forward with people or turning away from them, but seeing who they were, entirely, every complicated corner. And seeing *yourself,* too, as clear as ice on a pond. I was Kate McAllister when I saved Haddie Marks, and I was still Kate McAllister as I dribbled down that basketball court. The same in some ways, and different in others.

My world sure wasn't perfect.

But it was, in so many imperfect moments, blindingly, beautifully great.

ACKNOWLEDGMENTS

God doesn't need me to thank Him, but I'll do it anyway: may I never forget who gives me the people I'm thankful for.

Thank you to my very own A-team, Alyssa Miele and Alex Slater: thanks for championing me from the beginning. Your time and care and pep talks make my job infinitely more fun and rewarding.

Thank you, also, to the rest of the HarperCollins team, including Rosemary Brosnan, Lauren Levite, Lindsay Wagner, Maya Myers, and everyone else who brought Kate's story to life.

Richie Pope created this beautiful cover—you captured Kate perfectly!

Thank you to Tyler Saxton and the Brookfield girls' basketball summer camp for letting me tag along for a couple of days—go Spartans!

Immense gratitude to all my former classmates who I somehow survived middle school with—thank you for allowing me to comb through my memories and paint the scenes of East Middle. And a big ol' thank you to

Kristi Weimerskirch, without whom I never would have made it.

Thank you to Emily Irvine for playing with my kids so that I can actually get an hour to write!

Once again, the vast majority of this book was written at Café de Arts in Sussex, Wisconsin—thanks for your endless hospitality, Serena!

Many thanks to the friends in my corner who I can panic-text when working-mom life is getting the best of me: Jenny Parulski, Terri Meyerhofer, Michelle Gionet, Amanda Felsman, Leah Landrie, Kate Lawton, and Sam Povlock keep me grounded. Erica Comitalo, thank you for always being the first person I text when I see something related to MLMs. Emily Linn, your faith is awe-inspiring, and your friendship is priceless.

Kate doesn't have any siblings, but I do, and they are the best hype squad a girl could ask for. Paul, Mary Grace, John, Jenna, Ellie, Cole, and Asia: best life check, being your sister? Check. And my sweet niece, Nora Courchane: I love you more than you love chicken nuggets.

To my parents, Mark and Grace Courchane: thank you for being all the best parts of Sam and Casey and none of the bad. I could give thanks every day for your endless support, and it still wouldn't be enough. And thanks for the height (I guess).

Teresa and Benjamin: you remind me who I am.

And Krzysztof: you remind me whose I am.